THE NOVELS, STORIES
AND SKETCHES OF
F. HOPKINSON SMITH

L AGUERRE'S AND
WELL-WORN ROADS

CHARLES SCRIBNER'S
SONS ❦ NEW YORK ❦ 1902

*Published under special arrangement
with Houghton, Mifflin & Co.*

INTRODUCTION TO THE BEACON EDITION

WITH the publication of the Beacon Edition a word of explanation regarding the arrangement of my several works may perhaps spare the reader some confusion.

While the longer novels, "Tom Grogan," "Caleb West," and "Oliver Horn," are issued under separate covers as they were originally published, the shorter stories and sketches have been combined under different headings: those of Southern life being grouped with "Colonel Carter;" those of travel and adventure with "The White Umbrella in Mexico;" and those of Venetian life with "Gondola Days."

Changes have also been made in the tables of contents of "Well-worn Roads," "A Gentleman Vagabond," "A Day at Laguerre's," "Gondola Days," and "The Other Fellow," the full contents of these five volumes being

v

included in this edition, but rearranged to better express the general sentiment of the title story in each volume. Thus, "Between Showers in Dort" is part of the "A Day at Laguerre's" series, while "Captain Joe" and "John Sanders" and similar stories will be found in "The Other Fellow," a title which liberally translated means that under dog — that self-sacrificing and often sacrificed "other fellow" — whom we often forget either to thank or recognize or honor.

There have also been added to this Edition, under the sub-title of "Tile Club Stories," a number of sketches which have not yet appeared in any regular edition of my books.

The present sequence of the volumes comes as near as possible to the chronological order in which the several novels and stories were first published.

To my publishers I should like to express my grateful thanks for the beautiful dress in which they have clothed my stories.

F. H. S.

New York, March 13th, 1902.

CONTENTS

vii

CONTENTS

ILLUSTRATIONS

A DAY AT LAGUERRE'S

AND OTHER DAYS

INTRODUCTION

THESE slight sketches are the records of many idle days, stolen, I must confess, from a busy and far more practical life. I have committed these depredations upon myself for years, and have then run off to the far corners of the earth and sat down in some forgotten nook to enjoy my plunder.

The villany, strange to say, has only served to open my eyes the wider — and my heart too, for that matter — and to bring me closer to many fellow tramps who have delighted my soul, and still do.

Idle tramps if you will, who love the sunlight and simple fare and simple ways; ne'er-do-weels who haunt the cafés and breakfast at twelve; vagrants made millionaires by a melon and a cigarette; mendicants who own a donkey and a pair of panniers, have three feast days a week, earn but half a handful of copper coin, and sing all day for the very joy of living.

If you too can unhook your neck from the new car of Juggernaut — American Progress —

which is crushing out the sweetness of an old-time, simpler life, and would gain a little freedom, turn bandit yourself. If you have the pluck to take a long rest, the sun is still shining between showers in Dort. If you can only muster up courage for a short breathing spell, — even a day, — there is still a chop to be served under the vines overhanging the Bronx.

The stories are all true. Many of the names are genuine, and everybody is still alive. Most of them will be waiting for me when I run off again.

F. H. S.

New York, March, 1892.

A DAY AT LAGUERRE'S

IT is the most delightful of French inns, in the quaintest of French settlements. As you rush by in one of the innumerable trains that pass it daily, you may catch glimpses of tall trees trailing their branches in the still stream, — hardly a dozen yards wide, — of flocks of white ducks paddling together, and of queer punts drawn up on the shelving shore or tied to soggy, patched-up landing-stairs.

If the sun shines, you can see, now and then, between the trees, a figure kneeling at the water's edge, bending over a pile of clothes, washing, — her head bound with a red hand-kerchief.

If you are quick, the miniature river will open just before you round the curve, disclosing in the distance groups of willows, and a rickety foot-bridge perched up on poles to keep it dry. All this you see in a flash.

But you must stop at the old-fashioned station, within ten minutes of the Harlem River, cross the road, skirt an old garden bound with

5

a fence and bursting with flowers, and so pass on through a bare field to the water's edge, before you catch sight of the cosy little houses lining the banks, with garden fences cutting into the water, the arbors covered with tangled vines, and the boats crossing back and forth.

I have a love for the out-of-the-way places of the earth when they bristle all over with the quaint and the old and the odd, and are mouldy with the picturesque. But here is an in-the-way place, all sunshine and shimmer, with never a fringe of mould upon it, and yet you lose your heart at a glance. It is as charming in its boat life as an old Holland canal; it is as delightful in its shore life as the Seine; and it is as picturesque and entrancing in its sylvan beauty as the most exquisite of English streams.

The thousands of workaday souls who pass this spot daily in their whirl out and in the great city may catch all these glimpses of shade and sunlight over the edges of their journals, and any one of them living near the city's centre, with a stout pair of legs in his knickerbockers and the breath of the morning in his heart, can reach it afoot any day before breakfast; and yet not one in a hundred knows that this ideal nook exists.

Even this small percentage would be apt to

6

tell of the delights of Devonshire and of the
charm of the upper Thames, with its tall rushes
and low-thatched houses and quaint bridges,
as if the picturesque ended there ; forgetting
that right here at home there wanders many a
stream with its breast all silver that the trees
curtsy to as it sings through meadows waist-
high in lush grass, — as exquisite a picture as
can be found this beautiful land over.

So, this being an old tramping-ground of mine,
I have left the station with its noise and dust
behind me this lovely morning in June, have
stopped long enough to twist a bunch of sweet
peas through the garden fence, and am standing
on the bank waiting for some sign of life at
Madame Laguerre's. I discover that there is no
boat on my side of the stream. But that is of
no moment. On the other side, within a bis-
cuit's toss, so narrow is it, there are two boats;
and on the landing-wharf, which is only a few
planks wide, supporting a tumbledown flight of
steps leading to a vine-covered terrace above,
rest the oars.

I lay my traps down on the bank and begin
at the top of my voice : —

"Madame Laguerre ! Madame Laguerre !
Send Lucette with the boat."

For a long time there is no response. A young

7

girl drawing water a short distance below, hear-
ing my cries, says she will come ; and some
children above, who know me, begin paddling
over. I decline them all. Experience tells me
it is better to wait for madame.

In a few minutes she pushes aside the leaves,
peers through, and calls out : —

" Ah ! it is that horrible painter. Go away !
I have nothing for you. You are hungry again
that you come ? "

" Very, madame. Where is Lucette ? "

" Lucette ! Lucette ! It is always Lucette.
Luc-e-t-t-e ! " This in a shrill key. " It is the
painter. Come quick."

I have known Lucette for years, even when
she was a barefooted little tangle-hair, peeping
at me with her great brown eyes from beneath
her ragged straw hat. She wears high-heeled
slippers now, and sometimes on Sundays dainty
silk stockings, and her hair is braided down her
back, little French Marguérite that she is, and
her hat is never ragged any more, nor her hair
tangled. Her eyes, though, are still the same
velvety, half-drooping eyes, always opening and
shutting and never still.

As she springs into the boat and pulls towards
me I note how round and trim she is, and before
we have landed at Madame Laguerre's feet I

have counted up Lucette's birthdays, — those
that I know myself, — and find to my surprise
that she must be eighteen. We have always
been the best of friends, Lucette and I, ever
since she looked over my shoulder years ago
and watched me dot in the outlines of her boat,
with her dog Mustif sitting demurely in the
bow.

Madame, her mother, begins again : —

"Do you know that it is Saturday that you
come again to bother ? Now it will be a *filet*,
of course, with mushrooms and tomato salad ;
and there are no mushrooms, and no tomatoes,
and nothing. You are horrible. Then, when I
get it ready, you say you will come at three.
'Yes, madame ; at three,' — mimicking me, —
'sure, very sure.' But it is four, five, o'clock
— and then everything is burned up waiting.
Ah ! I know you."

This goes on always, and has for years. Pre-
sently she softens, for she is the most tender-
hearted of women, and would do anything in
the world to please me.

"But, then, you will be tired, and of course
you must have something. I remember now
there is a chicken. How will the chicken do ?
Oh, the chicken it is lovely, *charmant*. And
some pease — fresh. Monsieur picked them him-

9

self this morning. And some Roquefort, with an olive. Ah! You leave it to me ; but at three — no later — not one minute. *Sacré! Vous êtes le diable!*"

As we walk under the arbor and by the great trees, towards the cottage, Lucette following with the oars, I inquire after monsieur, and find that he is in the city, and very well and very busy, and will return at sundown. He has a shop of his own in the upper part where he makes *passe-partouts*. Here, at his home, madame maintains a simple restaurant for tramps like me.

These delightful people are old friends of mine, François Laguerre and his wife and their only child Lucette. They have lived here for nearly a quarter of a century. He is a straight, silver-haired old Frenchman of sixty, who left Paris, between two suns, nearly forty years ago, with a gendarme close at his heels, a red cockade under his coat, and an intense hatred in his heart for that "little nobody," Napoleon III.

If you met him on the boulevard you would look for the decoration on his lapel, remarking to yourself, "Some retired officer on half pay." If you met him at the railway station opposite you would say, "A French professor returning to his school." Both of these surmises are partly

wrong, and both partly right. Monsieur Laguerre has had a history. One can see by the
deep lines in his forehead and by the firm set of
his eyes and mouth that it has been an event-
ful one.

His wife is a few years his junior, short and
stout, and thoroughly French down to the very
toes of her felt slippers. She is devoted to François and Lucette, the best of cooks, and, in spite
of her scoldings, good-nature itself. As soon as
she hears me calling there arise before her the
visions of many delightful dinners prepared for
me by her own hand and ready to the minute
— all spoiled by my belated sketches. So she
begins to scold before I am out of the boat, or
in it, for that matter.

Across the fence next to Laguerre's lives a
confrère, a brother exile, Monsieur Marmosette,
who also has a shop in the city, where he carves
fine ivories. Monsieur Marmosette has only one
son. He too is named François, after his father's
old friend. Farther down on both sides of the
narrow stream front the cottages of other friends,
all Frenchmen ; and near the propped-up bridge
an Italian who knew Garibaldi burrows in a
low, slanting cabin, which is covered with vines.
I remember a dish of *spaghetti* under those vines,
and a flask of Chianti from its cellar, all cob-

webs and plaited straw, that left a taste of Venice in my mouth for days.

As there is only the great bridge above, which helps the country road across the little stream, and the little foot-bridge below, and as there is no path or road, — all the houses fronting the water, — the Bronx here is really the only highway, and so everybody must needs keep a boat. This is why the stream is crowded in the warm afternoons with all sorts of water crafts loaded with whole families, even to the babies, taking the air, or crossing from bank to bank in their daily pursuits.

There is a quality which one never sees in nature until she has been rough-handled by man and has outlived the usage. It is the picturesque. In the deep recesses of the primeval forest, along the mountain-slope, and away up the tumbling brook, nature may be majestic, beautiful, and even sublime; but she is never picturesque. This quality comes only after the axe and the saw have let the sunlight into the dense tangle and have scattered the falling timber, or the round of the water-wheel has divided the rush of the brook. It is so here. Some hundred years ago, along this quiet, silvery stream were encamped the troops of the struggling colonies, and, later, the great estates of the survivors stretched on each side for miles. The willows that now fringe these banks were saplings then ; and they and the great butternuts were only spared because their arching limbs shaded the cattle knee-deep along the shelving banks.

Then came the long interval that succeeds that deadly conversion of the once sweet farming lands, redolent with clover, into that barren waste — suburban property. The conflict that had lasted since the days when the pioneer's axe first rang through the stillness of the forest was nearly over ; nature saw her chance, took courage, and began that regeneration which is exclusively her own. The weeds ran riot ; tall grasses shot up into the sunlight, concealing the once well-trimmed banks ; and great tangles of underbrush and alders made lusty efforts to hide the traces of man's unceasing cruelty. Lastly came this little group of poor people from the Seine and the Marne and lent a helping hand, bringing with them something of their old life at home, — their boats, rude landings, patched-up water-stairs, fences, arbors, and vine-covered cottages, — unconsciously completing the picture and adding the one thing needful — a human touch. So nature, having outlived the wrongs of a hundred years, has here with busy

13

fingers so woven a web of weed, moss, trailing
vine, and low-branching tree that there is seen
a newer and more entrancing quality in her
beauty, which, for want of a better term, we
call the picturesque.

But madame is calling that the big boat must
be bailed out; that if I am ever coming back to
dinner it is absolutely necessary that I should go
away.

This boat is not of extraordinary size. It
is called the big boat from the fact that it has
one more seat than the one in which Lucette
rowed me over; and not being much in use except on Sunday, is generally half full of water.
Lucette insists on doing the bailing. She has
very often performed this service, and I have
always considered it as included in the curious
scrawl of a bill which madame gravely presents
at the end of each of my days here, beginning in
small printed type with "François Laguerre,
Restaurant Français," and ending with "Coffee
10 cents."

But this time I resist, remarking that she will
hurt her hands and soil her shoes, and that it
is all right as it is.

To this François the younger, who is leaning
over the fence, agrees, telling Lucette to wait
until he gets a pail.

14

Lucette catches his eye, colors a little, and says she will fetch it.

There is a break in the palings through which they both disappear, but I am halfway out on the stream, with my traps and umbrella on the seat in front and my coat and waistcoat tucked under the bow, before they return.

For half a mile down-stream there is barely a current. Then comes a break of a dozen yards just below the perched-up bridge, and the stream divides, one part rushing like a mill-race, and the other spreading itself softly around the roots of leaning willows, oozing through beds of water-plants, and creeping under masses of wild grapes and underbrush. Below this is a broad pasture fringed with another and larger growth of willows. Here the weeds are breast high, and in early autumn they burst into purple asters, and white immortelles, and goldenrod, and flaming sumac.

If a painter had a lifetime to spare, and loved this sort of material, — the willows, hillsides, and winding stream, — he would grow old and weary before he could paint it all ; and yet no two of his compositions need be alike. I have tied my boat under these same willows for ten years back, and I have not yet exhausted one corner of this neglected pasture,

15

There may be those who go a-fishing and enjoy it. The arranging and selecting of flies, the joining of rods, the prospective comfort in high water-boots, the creel with the leather strap, — every crease in it a reminder of some day without care or fret, — all this may bring the flush to the cheek and the eager kindling of the eye, and a certain sort of rest and happiness may come with it ; but — they have never gone a-sketching ! Hauled up on the wet bank in the long grass is your boat, with the frayed end of the painter tied around some willow that offers a helping root. Within a stone's throw, under a great branching of gnarled trees, is a nook where the curious sun, peeping at you through the interlaced leaves, will stencil Japanese shadows on your white umbrella. Then the trap is unstrapped, the stool opened, the easel put up, and you set your palette. The critical eye with which you look over your brush-case and the care with which you try each feather point upon your thumb-nail are but an index of your enjoyment.

Now you are ready. You loosen your cravat, hang your coat to some rustic peg in the creviced bark of the tree behind you, seize a bit of charcoal from your bag, sweep your eye around, and dash in a few guiding strokes.

Above is a turquoise sky filled with soft white clouds; behind you the great trunks of the many-branched willows; and away off, under the hot sun, the yellow-green of the wasted pasture, dotted with patches of rock and weeds, and hemmed in by the low hills that slope to the curving stream.

It is high noon. There is a stillness in the air that impresses you, broken only by the low murmur of the brook behind and the ceaseless song of the grasshopper among the weeds in front. A tired bumblebee hums past, rolls lazily over a clover blossom at your feet, and has his midday luncheon. Under the maples near the river's bend stands a group of horses, their heads touching. In the brook below are the patient cattle, with patches of sunlight gilding and bronzing their backs and sides. Every now and then a breath of cool air starts out from some shaded retreat, plays around your forehead, and passes on. All nature rests. It is her noontime.

But you work on: an enthusiasm has taken possession of you; the paints mix too slowly; you use your thumb, smearing and blending with a bit of rag — anything for the effect. One moment you are glued to your seat, your eye riveted on your canvas; the next, you are

17

up and backing away, taking it in as a whole, then pouncing down upon it quickly, belaboring it with your brush. Soon the trees take shape; the sky forms become definite; the meadow lies flat and loses itself in the fringe of willows.

When all of this begins to grow upon your once blank canvas, and some lucky pat matches the exact tone of blue-gray haze or shimmer of leaf, or some accidental blending of color delights you with its truth, a tingling goes down your backbone, and a rush surges through your veins that stirs you as nothing else in your whole life will ever do. The reaction comes the next day when, in the cold light of your studio, you see how far short you have come and how crude and false is your best touch compared with the glory of the landscape in your mind and heart. But the thrill that it gave you will linger forever.

But I hear a voice behind me calling out : —

"Monsieur, mamma says that dinner will be ready in half an hour. Please do not be late."

It is Lucette. She and François have come down in the other boat — the one with the little seat. They have moved so noiselessly that I have not even heard them. The sketch is

18

nearly finished ; and so, remembering the good
madame, and the Roquefort, and the olives, and
the many times I have kept her waiting, I wash
my brushes at once, throw my traps into the
boat, and pull back through the winding turn,
François taking the mill-race, and in the swift-
est part springing to the bank and towing Lucette, who sits in the stern, her white skirts
tucked around her dainty feet.

"*Sacré!* He is here. *C'est merveilleux!*
Why did you come ? "

" Because you sent for me, madame, and I
am hungry."

"*Mon Dieu!* He is hungry, and no
chicken ! "

It is true. The chicken was served that
morning to another tramp for breakfast, and
madame had forgotten all about it, and had ransacked the settlement for its mate. She was
too honest a cook to chase another into the fry-
ing-pan.

But there was a *filet* with mushrooms, and a
most surprising salad of chicory fresh from the
garden, and the pease were certain, and the
Roquefort and the olives beyond question. All
this she tells me as I walk past the table covered with a snow-white cloth and spread under
the grapevines overlooking the stream, with

19

the trees standing against the sky, their long shadows wrinkling down into the water.

I enter the summer kitchen built out into the garden, which also covers the old well, let down the bucket, and then, taking the clean crash towel from its hook, place the basin on the bench in the sunlight, and plunge my head into the cool water. Madame regards me curiously, her arms akimbo, re-hangs the towel, and asks : —

"Well, what about the wine ? The same ? "

"Yes ; but I will get it myself."

The cellar is underneath the larger house. Outside is an old-fashioned, sloping double door. These doors are always open, and a cool smell of damp straw flavored with vinegar from a leaky keg greets you as you descend into its recesses. On the hard earthen floor rest eight or ten great casks. The walls are lined with bottles large and small, loaded on shelves to which little white cards are tacked giving the vintage and brand. In one corner, under the small window, you will find dozens of boxes of French delicacies — truffles, pease, mushrooms, pâté de foie gras, mustard, and the like, and behind them rows of olive oil and olives. I carefully draw out a bottle from the row on the last shelf nearest the corner, mount the

steps, and place it on the table. Madame ex-
amines the cork, and puts down the bottle, remarking sententiously : —

" Château Lamonte, '62 ! Monsieur has told
you."

There may be ways of dining more delicious
than out in the open air under the vines in the
cool of the afternoon, with Lucette, in her whit-
est of aprons, flitting about, and madame gar-
nishing the dishes each in turn, and there may
be better bottles of honest red wine to be found
up and down this world of care than " Château
Lamonte, '62," but I have not yet discovered
them.

Lucette serves the coffee in a little cup, and
leaves the Roquefort and the cigarettes on the
table just as the sun is sinking behind the hill
skirting the railroad. While I am blowing rings
through the grape leaves over my head a quick
noise is heard across the stream. Lucette runs
past me through the garden, picking up her
oars as she goes.

" *Oui, mon père.* I am coming."

It is monsieur from his day's work in the
city.

"Who is here ? " I hear him say as he
mounts the terrace steps. " Oh, the painter —
good ! "

"Ah, *mon ami*. So you must see the willows once more. Have you not tired of them yet ? " Then, seating himself, "I hope madame has taken good care of you. What, the '62 ? Ah, I remember I told you."

When it is quite dark he joins me under the leaves, bringing a second bottle, a little better corked he thinks, and the talk drifts into his early life.

"What year was that, monsieur ? " I asked.

"In 1849. I was a young fellow just grown. I had learned my trade in Rheims, and I had come down to Paris to make my bread. Two years later came the little affair of December 2. That 'nobody,' Louis, had dissolved the National Assembly and the Council of State, and had issued his address to the army. Paris was in a ferment. By the help of his soldiers and police he had silenced every voice in Paris except his own. He had suppressed all the journals, and locked up everybody who had opposed him. Victor Hugo was in exile, Louis Blanc in London, Changarnier and Cavaignac in prison. At the moment I was working in a little shop near the Porte St. Martin decorating lacquerwork. We workmen all belonged to a secret society which met nightly in a back room over a wineshop near the Rue Royale. We had

but one thought — how to upset the little devil
at the Elysée. Among my comrades was a big
fellow from my own city, one Cambier. He
was the leader. On the ground floor of the
shop was built a huge oven where the lacquer
was baked. At night this was made hot with
charcoal and allowed to cool off in the morning,
ready for the finished work of the previous day.
It was Cambier's work to attend to this oven.

"One night just after all but he and two
others had left the shop, a strange man was discovered in a closet where the men kept their
working clothes. He was seized, brought to the
light, and instantly recognized as a member of
the secret police.

"At daylight the next morning I was aroused
from my bed, and, looking up, saw Chapot, an
inspector of police, standing over me. He had
known me from a boy, and was a friend of my
father's.

"'François, there is trouble at the shop. A
police agent has been murdered. His body was
found in the oven. Cambier is under arrest. I
know what you have been doing, but I also
know that in this you have had no hand. Here
are one hundred francs. Leave Paris in an
hour.'

"I put the money in my pocket, tied my

clothes in a bundle, and that night was on my way to Havre, and the next week set sail for here."

"And what became of Cambier?" I asked.

"I have never heard from that day to this, so I think they must have snuffed him out."

Then he drifted into his early life here — the weary tramping of the streets day after day, the half-starving result, the language and people unknown. Suddenly, somewhere in the lower part of the city, he espied a card tacked outside of a window bearing this inscription, "Decorator wanted." A man inside was painting one of the old-fashioned iron tea-trays common in those days. Monsieur took off his hat, pointed to the card, then to himself, seized the brush, and before the man could protest had covered the bottom with morning-glories so pink and fresh that his troubles ended on the spot. The first week he earned six dollars; but then this was to be paid at the end of it. For these six days he subsisted on one meal a day. This he ate at a restaurant where at night he washed dishes and blacked the head waiter's boots. When Saturday came, and the money was counted out in his hand, he thrust it into his pocket, left the shop, and sat down on a door-step outside to think.

24

"And, *mon ami,* what did I do first ? "

"Got something to eat ? "

"Never. I paid for a bath, had my hair cut and my face shaved, bought a shirt and collar, and then went back to the restaurant where I had washed dishes the night before, and the head waiter *served me.* After that it was easy ; the next week it was ten dollars ; then in a few years I had a place of my own ; then came madame and Lucette — and here we are."

The twilight had faded into a velvet blue, sprinkled with stars. The lantern which madame had hung against the arbor shed a yellow light, throwing into clear relief the sharply cut features of monsieur. Up and down the silent stream drifted here and there a phantom boat, the gleam of its light following like a firefly. From some came no sound but the muffled plash of the oars. From others floated stray bits of song and laughter. Far up the stream I heard the distant whistle of the down train.

"It is mine, monsieur. Will you cross with me, and bring back the boat ? "

Monsieur unhooked the lantern, and I followed through the garden and down the terrace steps.

At the water's edge was a bench holding two figures.

Monsieur turned his lantern, and the light fell upon the face of young François.

When the bow grated on the opposite bank I shook his hand, and said in parting, pointing to the lovers, —

" The same old story, monsieur ? "

" Yes ; and always new. You must come to the church."

ALONG THE BRONX

HIDDEN in our memories there are quaint, quiet nooks tucked away at the end of leafy lanes ; still streams overhung with feathery foliage ; gray rocks lichen-covered ; low-ground meadows, knee-deep in lush grass ; restful, lazy lakes dotted with pond-lilies; great, widespreading trees, their arms uplifted in song, their leaves quivering with the melody.

I say there are all these delights of leaf, moss, ripple, and shade stored away somewhere in our memories, — dry bulbs of a preceding summer's bloom, that need only the first touch of spring, the first glorious day in June, to break out into flower. When they do break out, they are generally chilled in the blooming by the thousand and one difficulties of prolonged travel, time of getting there and time of getting back again, expense, and lack of accommodations.

If you live in New York — and really you should not live anywhere else ! — there are a few buttons a tired man can touch that will revive for him all these delights in half an hour's walk, costing but a car-fare, and robbing no man or woman of time, even without the benefits of the eight-hour law.

You touch one of these buttons when you plan to spend an afternoon along the Bronx.

There are other buttons, of course. You can call up the edges of the Palisades, with their great sweep of river below, the seething, stream-ing city beyond ; or you can say " Hello ! " to the Upper Harlem, with its house-boats and floating restaurants ; or you can ring up West-chester and its picturesque water-line. But you cannot get them all together in half an hour except in one place, and that is along the Bronx.

The Bronx is the forgotten, the overlooked, the " disremembered," as the provincial puts it. Somebody may know where it begins — I do not. I only know where it ends. What its early life may be, away up near White Plains, what farms it waters, what dairies it cools, what herds it refreshes, I know not. I only know that when I get off at Woodlawn — that City of the Silent — it comes down from somewhere up above the railroad station, and that it " takes a header," as the boys say, under an old mill, abandoned long since, and then, like another idler, goes singing along through open meadows,

28

and around big trees in clumps, their roots washed bare, and then over sandy stretches reflecting the flurries of yellow butterflies, and then around a great hill, and so on down to Laguerre's.

Of course, when it gets to Laguerre's I know all about it. I know the old rotting landing wharf where monsieur moors his boats, — the one with the little seat is still there ; and Lucette's big eyes are just as brown, and her hair just as black, and her stockings and slippers just as dainty on Sundays as when first I knew her. And the wooden bench is still there, where the lovers used to sit ; only monsieur, her father, tells me that François works very late in the big city, — three mouths to feed now, you see, — and only when le petit François is tucked away in his crib in the long summer nights, and Lucette has washed the dishes and put on her best apron, and the Bronx stops still in a quiet pool to listen, is the bench used as in the old time when monsieur discovered the lovers by the flash of his lantern.

Then I know where it floats along below Laguerre's and pulls itself together in a very dignified way as it sails under the brand-new bridge, — the old one propped up on poles has long since paid tribute to a spring freshet, —

and quickens its pace below the old Dye-house, also a wreck now (they say it is haunted), and then goes slopping along in and out of the marshes, sousing the sunken willow roots, oozing through beds of weeds and tangled vines.

But only a very little while ago did I know where it began to leave off all its idle ways and took really to the serious side of life : rushing down long, stony ravines, plunging over respectable, well-to-do masonry dams, skirting once costly villas, whispering between dark defiles of rock, and otherwise disporting itself as becomes a well-ordered, conventional, self-respecting mountain stream, — uncontaminated by the encroachments and frivolities of civilized life.

All this begins at Fordham. Not exactly at Fordham, for you must walk due east from the station for half a mile, climb a fence, and strike through the woods before you hear its voice and catch the gleam of its tumbling current.

They will all be there when you go — all the quaint nooks, all the delights of leaf, moss, ripple, and shade of your early memories. And in the half-hour, too, — less if you are quick-footed, — from your desk or shop in the great city.

No, you never heard of it. I knew that be-

fore you said a word. You thought it was the
dumping-ground of half the cast-off tinware of
the earth ; that only the shanty, the hen-coop,
and the stable overhung its sluggish waters,
and only the carpet-shaker, the sod-gatherer,
and the tramp infested its banks.

I tell you that in all my wanderings in search
of the picturesque, nothing within a day's journey is half as charming. That its stretches of
meadow, willow clumps, and tangled densities
are as lovely, fresh, and enticing as can be
found — yes, within a thousand miles of your
door. That the rocks are encrusted with the
thickest of moss and lichen, gray, green, black,
and brilliant emerald. That the trees are superb, the solitude and rest complete. That it is
finer, more subtle, more exquisite than its sister brooks in the denser forest, because that
here and there it shows the trace of some human touch, — and nature is never truly picturesque without it, — the broken-down fence, the
sagging bridge, and the vine-covered roof.

But you must go *now*.

Now, before the grip of the great city has been
fastened upon it ; before the axe of the " dago "
clears out the wilderness of underbrush ; before
the landscape gardener, the sanitary engineer,
and the contractor pounce upon it and strangle

it; before the crimes of the cast-iron fountain, the varnished grapevine arbor, with seats to match, the bronze statues presented by admiring groups of citizens, the rambles, malls, and cement-lined caverns, are consummated; before the gravel walk confines your steps, and the granite curbing imprisons the flowers, as if they, too, would escape.

Now, when the tree lies as it falls; when the violets bloom and are there for the picking; when the dogwood sprinkles the bare branches with white stars, and the scent of the laurel fills the air.

Touch the button some day soon for an hour along the Bronx.

BETWEEN SHOWERS IN DORT

I

THERE be inns in Holland — not hotels, not pensions, nor stopping-places — just inns. The Bellevue at Dort is one, and the Holland Arms is another, and the — no, there are no others. Dort only boasts these two, and Dort to me is Holland.

The rivalry between these two inns has been going on for years, and it still continues. The Bellevue, fighting for place, elbowed its way years ago to the water-line, and took its stand on the river-front, where the windows and porticos could overlook the Maas dotted with boats. The Arms, discouraged, shrank back into its corner, and made up in low windows, smoking-rooms, and private bathroom — one for the whole house — what was lacking in porticos and sea view. Then followed a slight skirmish in paint, — red for the Arms and yellow-white for the Bellevue; and a flank movement of shades and curtains, — linen for the Arms and lace for the Bellevue. Scouting parties were

33

next ordered out, of porters in caps, banded with silk ribbons, bearing the names of their respective hostelries. Yacob of the Arms was to attack weary travellers on alighting from the train, and acquaint them with the delights of the downstairs bath, and the dark room for the kodakers, all free of charge. And Johan of the Bellevue was to give minute descriptions of the boats landing in front of the dining-room windows and of the superb view of the river.

It is always summer when I arrive in Dordrecht. I don't know what happens in winter, and I don't care. The groundhog knows enough to go into his hole when the snow begins to fly, and to stay there until the sun thaws him out again. Some tourists could profit by following his example.

It is summer, then, and the train has rolled into the station at Dordrecht, or beside it, and the traps have been thrown out, and Peter, my boatman — he of the " Red Tub," a craft with an outline like a Dutch vrou, quite as much beam as length (we go a-sketching in this boat) — Peter, I say, who has come to the train to meet me, has swung my belongings over his shoulder, and Johan, the porter of the Bellevue, with a triumphant glance at Yacob of the Arms,

34

has stowed the trunk on the rear platform of
the street tram, — no cabs or trucks, if you
please, in this town, — and the one-horse car
has jerked its way around short curves and up
through streets embowered in trees and paved
with cobblestones scrubbed as clean as china
plates, and over quaint bridges with glimpses of
sluggish canals and queer houses, and so on to
my lodgings.

And mine host, Heer Boudier, waiting on the
steps, takes me by the hand and says the same
room is ready and has been for a week.

Inside these two inns, the only inns in Dort,
the same rivalry exists. But my parallels must
cease. Mine own inn is the Bellevue, and my
old friend of fifteen years, Heer Boudier, is host,
and so loyalty compels me to omit mention of
any luxuries but those to which I am accustomed in his hostelry.

Its interior has peculiar charms for me. Scrupulously clean, simple in its appointments and
equipment, it is comfort itself. Tyne is respon-
sible for its cleanliness — or rather, that particular portion of Tyne which she bares above her
elbows. Nobody ever saw such a pair of sledge-
hammer arms as Tyne's on any girl outside of
Holland. She is eighteen; short, square-built,
solid as a Dutch cheese, fresh and rosy as an

35

English milkmaid; moon-faced, mild-eyed as
an Alderney heifer, and as strong as a three-
year-old. Her back and sides are as straight as
a plank; the front side is straight too. The
main joint in her body is at the hips. This is so
flexible that, wash-cloth in hand, she can lean
over the floor without bending her knees and
scrub every board in it till it shines like a Sunday dresser. She wears a snow-white cap as
dainty as the finest lady's in the land; an apron
that never seems to lose the crease of the iron,
and a blue print dress bunched up behind to
keep it from the slop. Her sturdy little legs are
covered by gray yarn stockings which she knits
herself, the feet thrust into wooden sabots.
These clatter over the cobbles as she scurries
about with a crab-like movement, sousing, dous-
ing, and scrubbing as she goes; for Tyne at-
tacks the sidewalk outside with as much gusto
as she does the hall and floors.

Johan the porter moves the chairs out of
Tyne's way when she begins work, and, lately,
I have caught him lifting her bucket up the
front steps — a wholly unnecessary proceeding
when Tyne's muscular developments are considered. Johan and I had a confidential talk
one night, when he brought the mail to my
room, — the room on the second floor over-

looking the Maas, — in which certain personal statements were made. When I spoke to Tyne about them the next day, she looked at me with her big blue eyes, and then broke into a laugh, opening her mouth so wide that every tooth in her head flashed white (they always reminded me somehow of peeled almonds). With a little bridling twist of her head she answered that — but, of course, this was a strictly confidential communication, and of so entirely private a nature that no gentleman under the circumstances would permit a single word of it to —

Johan is taller than Tyne, but not so thick through. When he meets you at the station, with his cap and band in his hand, his red hair trimmed behind as square as the end of a whisk-broom, his thin, parenthesis legs and Vienna guardsman waist, — each detail the very opposite, you will note, from Tyne's, — you recall immediately one of George Boughton's typical Dutchmen. The only thing lacking is his pipe; he is too busy for that.

When he dons his dress suit for dinner, and bending over your shoulder asks, in his best English : "Mynheer, don't it now de feesh you haf?" you lose sight of Boughton's Dutchman and see only the cosmopolitan. The transformation is due entirely to Continental influences —

Dort being one of the main highways between London and Paris — influences so strong that even in this water-logged town on the Maas, bonnets are beginning to replace caps, and French shoes sabots.

The guests that Johan serves at this inn of my good friend Boudier are as odd-looking as its interior. They line both sides and the two ends of the long table. Stout Germans in horrible clothes, with stouter wives in worse; Dutchmen from up-country in brown coats and green waistcoats; clerks off on a vacation with kodaks and Cook's tickets; bicyclists in knickerbockers; painters, with large kits and small handbags, who talk all the time and to everybody; gray-whiskered, red-faced Englishmen, with absolutely no conversation at all, who prove to be distinguished persons attended by their own valets, and on their way to Aix or the Engadine, now that the salmon-fishing in Norway is over; school teachers from America, just arrived from Antwerp or Rotterdam, or from across the channel by way of Harwich, their first stopping-place really since they left home — one travelling-dress and a black silk in the bag; all the kinds and conditions and sorts of people who seek out precious little places like Dort, either because they are cheap

38

or comfortable, or because they are known to be picturesque.

I sought out Dort years ago because it was untouched by the hurry that makes life miserable and the shams that make it vulgar, and I go back to it now every year of my life, in spite of other foreign influences.

And there is no real change in fifteen years. Its old trees still nod over the sleepy canals in the same sleepy way they have done, no doubt, for a century. The rooks — the same rooks, they never die — still swoop in and out of the weather-stained arches high up in the great tower of the Groote Kerk, the old twelfth-century church, the tallest in all Holland ; the big-waisted Dutch luggers with rudders painted arsenic green — what would painters do without this green ? — doze under the trees, their mooring lines tied to the trunks ; the girls and boys, with arms locked, a dozen together, clatter over the cobbles, singing as they walk ; the steamboats land and hurry on — " Fop Smit's boats " the signs read — it is pretty close, but I am not part owner in the line ; the gossips lean in the doorways or under the windows banked with geraniums and nasturtiums ; the cumbersome state carriages with the big ungainly horses with untrimmed manes and tails — there are

39

only five of these carriages in all Dordrecht —
wait in front of the great houses eighty feet
wide and four stories high, some dating as far
back as 1512, and still occupied by descendants
of the same families; the old women in ivory
black, with dabs of Chinese white for sabots
and caps, push the same carts loaded with
Hooker's green vegetables from door to door;
the town crier rings his bell; the watchman
calls the hour.

Over all bends the ever-changing sky, one
hour close-drawn, gray-lined, with slanting
slashes of blinding rain, the next piled high
with great domes of silver-white clouds inlaid
with turquoise blue or hemmed in by low-lying
ranges of purple peaks capped with gold.

.   .   .   .

I confess that an acute sense of disappointment came over me when I first saw these gray
canals, rain-varnished streets, and rows of green
trees. I recognized at a glance that it was not
my Holland; not the Holland of my dreams;
not the Holland of Mesdag nor Poggenbeck nor
Kever. It was a fresher, sweeter, more whole-
some land, and with a more breathable air.
These Dutch painters had taught me to look
for dull, dirty skies, soggy wharves, and dismal
perspectives of endless dykes. They had shown

40

THESE GRAY CANALS . . . AND ROWS OF GREEN TREES.

me countless windmills, scattered along stretches
of wind-swept moors backed by lowering skies,
cold gray streets, quaint, leanover houses, and
smudgy, grimy interiors. They had enveloped
all this in the stifling, murky atmosphere of a
Western city slowly strangling in clouds of coal
smoke.

These Dutch artists were, perhaps, not alone
in this falsification. It is one of the peculiarities
of modern art that many of its masters cater to
the taste of a public who want something that
is not in preference to something that *is*. Ziem,
for instance, had, up to the time of my enlight-
enment, taught me to love an equally untrue and
impossible Venice, — a Venice all red and yellow and deep ultramarine blue, a Venice of
unbuildable palaces and blazing red walls.

I do not care to say so aloud, where I can
be heard over the way, but if you will please
come inside my quarters, and shut the door,
and putty up the keyhole, and draw down the
blinds, I will whisper in your ear that my own
private opinion is that even Turner himself
would have been an infinitely greater artist had
he built his pictures on Venice instead of building them on Turner. I will also be courageous
enough to assert that the beauty and dignity of
Venetian architecture — an architecture which

has delighted many appreciative souls for centuries — finds no place in his canvases, either
in detail or in mass. The details may be unimportant, for the soft vapor of the lagoons oft-
times conceals them, but the correct outline of
the mass — that is, for instance, the true pro-
portion of the dome of the Salute, that incom-
parable, incandescent pearl, or the vertical line
of the Campanile compared to the roofs of the
connecting palaces — should never be ignored,
for they are as much a part of Venice, the part
that makes for beauty, as the shimmering light
of the morning or the glory of its sunsets. So it
is that when most of us for the first time reach
the water-gates of Venice, the most beautiful of
all cities by the sea, we feel a certain shock and
must begin to fall in love with a new sweetheart.

So with many painters of the Holland school
— not the old Dutch school of landscape painters, but the more modern group of men who
paint their native skies with zinc-white toned
with London fog, or mummy dust and bitumen.
It is all very artistic and full of "tone," but it
is not Holland.

There is Clays, for instance. Of all modern
painters Clays has charmed and wooed us best
with certain phases of Holland life, particularly

the burly brown boats lying at anchor, their red and white sails reflected in the water. I love these boats of Clays. They are superbly drawn, strong in color, and admirably painted ; the water treatment, too, is beyond criticism. But where are they in Holland ? I know Holland from the Zuyder Zee to Rotterdam, but I have never yet seen one of Clays's boats in the original wood.

Thus by reason of such smeary, up and down fairy tales in paint have we gradually become convinced that vague trees, and black houses with staring patches of whitewash, and Van-dyke brown roofs are thoroughly characteristic of Holland, and that the blessed sun never shines in this land of sabots.

But does n't it rain ? Yes, about half the time, perhaps three quarters of the time. Well, now that I think of it, about all the time. But not continuously ; only in intermittent down-pours, floods, gushes of water — not once a day, but every half hour. Then comes the quick drawing of a gray curtain from a wide expanse of blue, framing ranges of snow-capped cumuli ; streets swimming in great pools; drenched leaves quivering in dazzling sunlight, and millions of raindrops flashing like diamonds.

II

But Peter, my boatman, cap in hand, is
waiting on the cobbles outside the inn door. He
has served me these many years. He is a wiry,
thin, pinch-faced Dutchman, of perhaps sixty,
who spent his early life at sea as man-o'-war's-
man, common sailor, and then mate, and his
later years at home in Dort, picking up odd
jobs of ferriage or stevedoring, or making early
gardens. While on duty he wears an old white
travelling-cap pulled over his eyes, and a flannel shirt without collar or tie, and sail-maker's
trousers. These trousers are caught at his hips
by a leather strap supporting a sheath which
holds his knife. He cuts everything with this
knife, from apples and navy plug to ship's cables and telegraph wire. His clothes are water-
proof ; they must be, for no matter how hard
it rains, Peter is always dry. The water may
pour in rivulets from off his cap, and run down
his forehead and from the end of his gargoyle
of a nose, but no drop ever seems to wet his
skin. When it rains the fiercest, I, of course,
retreat under the poke-bonnet awning made of
cotton duck stretched over barrel hoops that
protects the stern of my boat, but Peter never
moves. This Dutch rain does not in any way

44

affect him. It is like the Jersey mosquito — it always spares the natives.

Peter speaks two languages, both Dutch. He says that one is English, but he cannot prove it — nobody can. When he opens his mouth you know all about his ridiculous pretensions. He says, "Mynheer, dot manus ist er blowdy rock." He has learned this expression from the English sailors unloading coal at the big docks opposite Pappendrecht, and he has incorporated thus much of their slang into his own nut-cracking dialect. He means of course "that man is a bloody rogue." He has a dozen other phrases equally obscure.

Peter's mission this first morning after my arrival is to report that the good ship Red Tub is now lying in the harbor fully equipped for active service. That her aft awning has been hauled taut over its hoops; that her lockers of empty cigar boxes (receptacles for brushes) have been clewed up; the cocoa-matting rolled out the whole length of her keel, and finally that the water bucket and wooden chair (I use a chair instead of an easel) have been properly stowed.

Before the next raincloud spills over its edges, we must loosen the painter from the iron ring rusted tight in the square stone in the wharf, man the oars, and creep under the little bridge

45

that binds Boudier's landing to the sidewalk over the way, and so set our course for the open Maas. For I am in search of Dutch boats to-day, as near like Clays's as I can find. I round the point above the old India warehouses, I catch sight of the topmasts of two old luggers anchored in midstream, their long red pennants flattened against the gray sky. The wind is fresh from the east, filling the sails of the big windmills blown tight against their whirling arms. The fishing-smacks lean over like dipping gulls ; the yellow water of the Maas is flecked with wavy lines of beer foam.

The good ship Red Tub is not adapted to outdoor sketching under these conditions. The poke-bonnet awning acts as a wind-drag that no amount of hard pulling can overcome. So I at once convene the Board of Strategy, Lieutenant - Commander Peter Jansen, Red Tub Navy, in the chair. That distinguished naval expert rises from his water-soaked seat on the cocoa-matting outside the poke bonnet, sweeps his eye around the horizon, and remarks sententiously : —

"It no tam goot day. Blow all dime ; we go ba'd-hoose," and he turns the boat toward a low-lying building anchored out from the main shore by huge chains secured to floating buoys.

46

BETWEEN SHOWERS IN DORT

In some harbors sea-faring men are warned not to "anchor over the water-pipes." In others particular directions are given to avoid "submarine cables planted here." In Dort, where none of these modern conveniences exist, you are notified as follows : "No boats must land at this Bath."

If Peter knew of this rule he said not one word to me as I sat back out of the wet, hived under the poke bonnet, squeezing color-tubes and assorting my brushes. He rowed our craft toward the bath-house with the skill of a man-o'-war's-man, twisted the painter around a short post, and unloaded my paraphernalia on a narrow ledge or plank walk some three feet wide, and which ran around the edge of the floating bath-house.

It never takes me long to get to work, once my subject is selected. I sprang from the boat while Peter handed me the chair, stool, and portfolio containing my stock of gray papers of different tones ; opened my sketch frame, caught a sheet of paper tight between its cleats ; spread palettes and brushes on the floor at my side ; placed the water bucket within reach of my hand, and in five minutes I was absorbed in my sketch.

Immediately the customary thing happened.

The big bank of gray cloud that hung over
the river split into feathery masses of white
framed in blue, and out blazed the glorious
sun.

Meantime, Peter had squatted close beside
me, sheltered under the lee of the side wall of
the bath-house, protected equally from the slant
of the driving rain and the glare of the blinding
sun. Safe too from the watchful eye of the
High Pan-Jam who managed the bath, and who
at the moment was entirely oblivious of the
fact that only two inches of pine board separated him from an enthusiastic painter working
like mad, and an equally alert marine assistant
who supplied him with fresh water and charcoal points, both at the moment defying the
law of the land, one in ignorance and the other
in a spirit of sheer bravado. For Peter must
have known the code and the penalty.

The world is an easy place for a painter to
live and breathe in when he is sitting far from
the madding crowd — of boys — protected from
the wind and sun, watching a sky piled up in
mountains of snow, and inhaling ozone that is
a tonic to his lungs. When the outline of his
sketch is complete and the colors flow and blend,
and the heart is on fire ; when the bare paper
begins to lose itself in purple distances and long

stretches of tumbling water, and the pictured boats take definite shape, and the lines of the rigging begin to tell ; when little by little, with a pat here and a dab there, there comes from out this flat space a something that thrilled him when he first determined to paint the thing that caught his eye, — not the thing itself, but the spirit, the soul, the feeling and meaning of the color poem unrolled before him, — when a painter feels a thrill like this, all the fleets of Spain might bombard him, and his eye would never waver nor his touch hesitate.

I felt it to-day.

Peter did n't. If he had he would have kept still and passed me fresh water and rags and new tubes and whatever I wanted — and I wanted something every minute — instead of disporting himself in an entirely idiotic and disastrous way. Disastrous, because you might have seen the sketch which I began reproduced in these pages had the Lieutenant-Commander, R. T. N., only carried out the orders of the Lord High Admiral commanding the fleet.

A sunbeam began it. It peeped over the edge of the side wall — the wall really was but little higher than Peter's head when he stood erect — and started in to creep down my half-finished sketch. Peter rose in his wrath, reached for my white umbrella, and at once opened it and screwed together the jointed handle. Then he began searching for some convenient supporting hook on which to hang his shield of defence. Next a brilliant, intellectual dynamite bomb of a thought split his cranium. He would hoist the umbrella *above* the top of the thin wall of the bath-house, resting one half upon its upper edge, drive the iron spike into the plank under our feet, and secure the handle by placing his back against it. No sunbeam should pass him!

The effect can be imagined on the High Pan-Jam inside the bath-house — an amphibious guardian, oblivious naturally to sun and rain — when his eye fell upon this flag of defiance thrust up above his ramparts. You can imagine, too, the consternation of the peaceful inmates of the open pools, whose laughter had now and then risen above the sough of the wind and splash of the water. Almost immediately I heard the sound of hurrying footsteps from a point whence no sound had come before, and there followed the scraping of a pair of toes on the planking behind me, as if some one was drawing himself up.

I looked around and up and saw eight fingers clutching the top of the planking, and a moment

later the round face of an astonished Dutchman.
I have n't the faintest idea what he said. I
did n't know then and I don't know now. I
only remember that his dialect sounded like
the traditional crackling of thorns under a pot,
including the sputtering, and suggesting the
equally heated temperature. When his fingers
gave out he would drop out of sight, only to rise
again and continue the attack.

Here Peter, I must say, did credit to his
Dutch ancestors. He did not temporize. He did
not argue. He ignored diplomacy at the start,
and blazed out that we were out of everybody's
way and on the lee side of the structure; that
there was no sign up on that side; that I was
a most distinguished personage of blameless life
and character, and that, rules or no rules, he
was going to stay where he was and so was I.

"You tam blowdy rock. It 's s'welve o'clook
now — no rule aft' s'welve o'clook — nopody
ba'd now; " this in Dutch, but it meant that,
then turning to me, "You stay — you no go —
I brek tam head him." —

None of this interested me. I had heard
Peter explode before. I was trying to match
the tone of an opalescent cloud inlaid with
mother-of-pearl, the shadow side all purplish
gray. Its warm high-lights came all right, but

51

I was half out of my head trying to get its shadow-tones true with Payne's gray and cobalt. The cloud itself had already cast its moorings and was fast drifting over the English Channel. It would be out of sight in five minutes.

"Peter — *Peter !* " I cried. " Don't talk so much. Here, give him half a gulden and tell him to dry up. Hand me that sky brush — quick now ! "

The High Pan-Jam dropped with a thud to his feet. His swinging footsteps could be heard growing fainter, but no stiver of my silver had lined his pocket.

I worked on. The tea-rose cloud had disappeared entirely ; only its poor counterfeit remained. The boats were nearly finished ; another wash over their sails would bring them all right. Then the tramp as of armed men came from the in-shore side of the bath-house. Peter stood up and craned his neck around the edge of the planking, and said in an undertone :

"Tam b'lice, he come now ; nev' mind, you stay 'ere — no go. Tam blowdy rock no mak' you go."

Behind me stood the High Pan-Jam who had scraped his toes on the fence. With him was an officer of police !

Peter was now stamping his feet, swearing

in Dutch, English, and polyglot, and threatening to sponge the Dutch government from the face of the universe.

My experience has told me that it is never safe to monkey with a gendarme. He is generally a perfectly cool, self-poised, unimpressionable individual, with no animosity whatever toward you or anybody else, but who intends to be obeyed, not because it pleases him, but because the power behind him compels it. I instantly rose from my stool, touched my hat in respectful military salute, and opened my cigarette-case. The gendarme selected a cigarette with perfect coolness and good humor, and began politely to unfold to me his duties in connection with the municipal laws of Dordrecht. The manager of the bath, he said, had invoked his services. I might not be aware that it was against the law to land on this side of the bath-house, etc.

But the blood of the Jansens was up. Some old Koop or De Witt or Von Somebody was stirring Peter.

"No ba'd aft' s'welve o'clook." This to me, both fists in the air, one perilously near the officer's face. The original invective was in his native tongue, hurled at Pan-Jam and the officer alike.

53

"What difference does it make, your Excellency," I asked, "whether I sit in my boat and paint or sit here where there is less motion?"

"None, honored sir," and he took a fresh cigarette (Peter was now interpreting), "except for the fact that you have taken up your position on the *women's* side of the bath-house. They bathe from twelve o'clock till four. When the ladies saw the umbrella they were greatly disturbed. They are now waiting for you to go away!"

III

My room at Heer Boudier's commands a full view of the Maas, with all its varied shipping. Its interior fittings are so scrupulously clean that one feels almost uncomfortable lest some of the dainty appointments might be soiled in the using. The bed is the most remarkable of all its comforts. It is more of a box than a bed, and so high at head and foot, and so solid at its sides, that it only needs a lid to make the comparison complete. There is always at its foot an inflated eider-down quilt puffed up like a French souffle potato; and there are always at its head two little oval pillows solid as bags of ballast, surmounting a bolster that slopes off to an edge. I have never yet found out what this

54

bolster is stuffed with. The bed itself would be
bottomless but for the slats. When you first
fall overboard into this slough you begin to sink
through its layers of feathers, and instinctively
throw out your hands, catching at the side
boards as a drowning man would clutch at the
gunwales of a suddenly capsized boat.

The second night after my arrival, I, in ac-
cordance with my annual custom, deposited the
contents of this bed in a huge pile outside my
door, making a bottom layer of the feathers,
then the bolster, and last the souffle with the
bags of ballast on top.

Then I rang for Tyne.

She had forgotten all about the way I liked
my sleeping arrangements until she saw the
pile of bedding. Then she held her sides with
laughter, while the tears streamed down her
red cheeks. Of course, the Heer should have
a mattress and big English pillows, and no
bouncy-bounce, speaking the words not with
her lips, but with a gesture of her hand. Then
she called Johan to help. I never can see why
Tyne always calls Johan to help when there is
anything to be done about my room out of the
usual order of things, — the sweeping, dusting,
etc., — but she does. I know full well that if
she so pleased she could tuck the whole pile of

55

bedding under her chin, pick up the bureau in one hand and the bed in the other, and walk downstairs without even mussing her cap-strings.

When Johan returned with a hair mattress and English pillows, — you can get anything you want at Boudier's, — he asked me if I had heard the news about Peter. Johan, by the way, speaks very good English — for Johan. The Burgomaster, he said, had that day served Peter with a writ. If I had looked out of the window an hour ago, I could have seen the Lieutenant-Commander of the Red Tub, under charge of an officer of the law, on his way to the Town Hall. Peter, he added, had just returned and was at the present moment engaged in scrubbing out the R. T. for active service in the morning.

I at once sent for Peter.

He came up, hat in hand. But there was no sign of weakening. The blood of the Jansens was still in his eye.

"What did they arrest you for, Peter?"

"For make jaw wid de tam bolice. He say I mos' pay two gulden or one tay in jail. Oh, it is notting; I no pay. Dot bolice lie ven he say vimmen ba'd. Nopoty ba'd in the hoose aft' s'welve 'clook."

Later, Heer Boudier tells me that because of

Peter's action in resisting the officer in the dis-
charge of his duty, he is under arrest, and that
he has but *five days in which to make up his
mind* as to whether he will live on bread and
water for a day and night in the town jail, or
whether he will deplete his slender savings in
favor of the state to the extent of two gulden.

"But don't they lock him up, meanwhile?"
I asked.

Boudier laughed. "Where would he run to,
and for what? to save two gulden?"

My heart was touched. I could not possibly
allow Peter to spend five minutes in jail on my
account. I should not have slept one wink
that night, even in my luxurious bedbox with
English pillows, knowing that the Lieutenant-
Commander was stretched out on a cold floor
with a cobblestone under his cheek. I knew,
too, how slender was his store, and what a godsend my annual visit had been to his butcher
and baker. The Commander of the Red Tub
might be impetuous, even aggressive, but by
no possible stretch of the imagination could he
be considered criminal.

That night I added these two gulden (about
eighty cents) to Peter's wages. He thanked
me with a pleased twinkle in his eye, and a
wrinkling of the leathery skin around his nose

and mouth. Then he put on his cap and disappeared up the street.

. . . .

But the inns, quaint canals, and rain-washed streets are not Dort's only distinctions. There is an ancient Groote Kerk, overlaid with colors that are rarely found outside of Holland. It is built of brick, with a huge square tower that rises above the great elms pressing close about it, and which is visible for miles. The moist climate not only encrusts its twelfth-century porch with brown-and-green patches of lichen over the red tones, but dims the great stained-glass windows with films of mould, and covers with streaks of Hooker's green the shadow sides of the long sloping roofs. Even the brick pavements about it are carpeted with strips of green, as fresh in color as if no passing foot had touched them. And few feet ever do touch them, for it is but a small group of worshippers that gather weekly within the old kirk's whitewashed walls.

These faithful few do not find the rich interior of the olden time, for many changes have come over it since its cathedral days, the days of its pomp and circumstance. All its old-time color is gone when you enter its portals, and only staring white walls and rigid, naked columns

58

remain ; only dull gray stone floors and hard, stiff-backed benches. I have often sat upon these same benches in the gloom of a fast-fading twilight and looked about me, bemoaning the bareness, and wondering what its *ensemble* must have been in the days of its magnificence. There is nothing left of its glories now but its architectural lines. The walls have been stripped of their costly velvets, tapestries, and banners of silk and gold ; the uplifted cross is gone ; the haze of swinging censers no longer blurs the vistas, nor the soft light of many tapers illumines their gloom.

I have always believed that duty and beauty should ever go hand in hand in our churches. To me there is nothing too rich in tone, too luxurious in color, too exquisite in line for the House of God. Nothing that the brush of the painter can make glorious, the chisel of the sculptor beautify, or the T-square of the architect ennoble, can ever be out of place in the one building of all others that we dedicate to the Creator of all beauty. I have always thanked Him for his goodness in giving as much thought to the flowers that cover the hillsides as He did to the dull earth that lies beneath ; as much care to the matchings of purples and gold in the sunsets as to the blue-black crags that are

59

outlined against them. With these feelings in my heart I have never understood that form of worship which contents itself with a bare barn filled with seats of pine, a square box of a pulpit, a lone pitcher of ice water, and a popular edition of the hymns. But then, I am not a Dutchman.

Besides this town of Dort, filled with queer warehouses, odd buildings, and cobbled streets, and dominated by this majestic cathedral, there is across the river — just a little way (Peter rows me over in ten minutes) — the Noah's Ark town of Pappendrecht, surrounded by great stretches of green meadow, dotted with black and white cows, and acres and acres of cabbages and garden truck, and tiny farmhouses, and absurdly big barns; and back of these, and in order to keep all these dry, is a big dyke that goes on forever and is lost in the perspective. On both sides of this dyke (its top is a road) are built the toy houses facing each other, each one cleaner and better scrubbed than its neighbor, their big windows gay with geraniums.

Farther down is another 'recht — I cannot for the life of me remember the first part of its name — where there is a shipyard and big windlasses and a horse hitched to a sweep, which winds up water-soaked luggers on to rude ways, and great pots of boiling tar, the yellow smoke drifting away toward the sea.

And between these towns of Dort, Pappendrecht, and the other 'recht moves a constant procession of water craft; a never-ceasing string of low, rakish barges that bear the commerce of Germany out to the sea, each in charge of a powerful tug puffing eagerly in its hurry to reach tide water, besides all the other boats and luggers that sail and steam up and down the forked Maas in front of Boudier's Inn — for Dort is really on an island, the water of the Rhine being divided here. You would never think, were you to watch these ungainly boats, that they could ever arrive anywhere. They look as if they were built to go sideways, endways, or both ways; and yet they mind their helms and dodge in and out and swoop past the long points of land ending in the waving marsh grass, and all with the ease of a steam yacht.

. . . .

These and a hundred other things make me love this quaint old town on the Maas. There is everything within its borders for the painter who loves form and color — boats, queer houses, streets, canals, odd, picturesque interiors, figures, brass milk cans, white-capped girls, and stretches of marsh. If there were not other places on the earth I love equally as well — Venice, for instance — I would be content never to leave its shower-drenched streets. But I know that my gondola, gay in its new *tenta* and polished brasses, is waiting for me in the little canal next the bridge, and I must be off.

Tyne has already packed my trunk, and Johan is ready to take it down the stairs. Tyne sent for him. I did not.

When Johan, like an overloaded burro stumbling down the narrow defile of the staircase, my trunk on his back, disappears through the lower door, Tyne reënters my room, closes the door softly, and tells me that Johan's wages have been raised, and that before I return next summer she and —

But I forgot. This is another strictly confidential communication. Under no possible circumstances could a man of honor — certainly not.

Peter, to my surprise, is not in his customary place when I reach the outer street door. Johan, at my inquiring gesture, grins the width of his face, but has no information to impart regarding Peter's unusual absence.

Heer Boudier is more explicit.

"Where's Peter?" I cry with some impatience.

My host shrugs his shoulders with a helpless movement, and opens wide the fingers of both hands.

"Mynheer, the five days are up. Peter has gone to jail."

"What for?" I ask in astonishment.

"To save two gulden."

AN ESCAPADE IN CORDOVA

THE first day he contented himself with merely glancing my way as I emerged from the door of my lodging, following me with his eyes until I disappeared around the corner of the narrow street that leads to the Moorish mosque.

Then he took to raising his hat with quite the air of a hidalgo, standing uncovered on the narrow sidewalk until I passed, expressing by this simple courtesy a sort of silent apology for occupying my premises.

I always returned his salute, wishing him "good-day" with great gusto, adding occasionally the desire that the good God would go with him during its sultry hours. Such graceful compliments tend to make life more enjoyable in old Spanish cities.

But he never addressed a word to me in reply, only bowed the lower, his eyes fixed upon mine, his whole manner suggestive of a wistful desire for closer acquaintanceship. To this was added a certain fearless independence which banished at once all thought of offering him alms.

I began to wonder who this very courteous, very silent, and very friendly young man might be. I began also to count over the various possible and impossible motives which might influence him to become a fixture on the right of my doorstep every morning when I started out with my empty sketch-trap.

It was plainly evident that he belonged to the better class of Spaniards, and not to "the people." You could see that in his finely chiselled features, and in the way his clothes, though slightly the worse for wear, fitted his graceful, slender figure. You saw it also in his winning mouth, full of white teeth, shaded by a dark mustache with just enough curl to suggest the Don Juan, — ready for fan, slipper, or blade. And yet with all this there was a certain air of sadness about him that enlisted your sympathy at sight.

The swarthy landlady who peered through the lattice-blinds had never seen him before, and expressed, rather pointedly, I thought, the hope that she never would again. The picador who during the bull-fights occupied a room on a floor above mine charged down upon him very much as he would on a wounded bull, and returned to me, waiting behind the half-open door, with a shrug of his broad shoulders, a lifting of his

eyebrows, and the single word, " Nada ! "
(good-for-nothing).

Still the silent young man continued to occupy
my sidewalk, to bow with his hat to the ground,
and to follow me with his eyes around the corner of the narrow street that led to the Moorish
mosque.

Then a break occurred in the daily programme.
I had forgotten my brush-case, and ran back to
the house, leaving my white umbrella and trap
on the doorstep. When I emerged again into
the blinding sunlight, they had disappeared. I
instinctively sought out my silent young man.
He was standing in his customary place, hat
off, my trap in one hand, — the umbrella under
his arm.

" My friend, you have my trap."

" Yes, señor."

" Why ? "

" It is too heavy for the painter. Let me
carry it."

His voice was so gentle, his face so honest,
his manner so courteous, his desire to serve me
so apparent, that I surrendered the brush-case
at once ; had it been filled with doubloons I
would have done the same.

" What is your name ? "

" Manuel."

"Why are you always here ? "

"To wait upon you."

" For what ? "

" To keep from starving."

"Have you had any breakfast ? "

"No ; nor supper."

Below the mosque there runs a crooked street lined with balconies hooded with awnings shading tropical plants, and now and then a pretty señorita. At the end of this street is an arcade flanking the old bull-ring. Through one of its arches you enter the best café in Cordova.

To see a hungry man eat has always been to me one of the most delightful of all the expositions of the laws of want and supply ; to assist in equalizing these laws the most exquisite of pleasures. I exhausted all my resources on Manuel.

He had a cup of coffee as big as a soup-bowl. He had an omelet crammed full of garlic. He had a pile of waffles smothered in sugar. He had chicken livers broiled in peppers and little round radishes, and a yard of bread, and, last of all, a flagon of San Vicente. All these he ate and drank with the air and manners of a gentleman, smoking a cigarette, as is the custom, throughout the entire repast, and talking to me of his life, — his people at home, his year at

the military school at Toledo, of the unfortu-
nate scrape which ended in his dismissal, of the
anger of his father, of the beauty and devotion
of the girl who caused it all, and of his coming
to Cordova to be near her. Who does not re-
collect his own shortcomings in the hot, foolish
days of his youth ? I could see it all ; hardly
twenty, straight as an arrow, lithe as a whip,
eyes coals of fire, cheeks like a rose, and his
veins packed full of blood at fever heat.

He had watched me painting in the plaza,
and had followed me to my lodgings, hoping I
would employ him to carry my trap, but had
been too timid to ask for it until chance threw
it in his way. He would be glad to carry it now
all day to pay for his breakfast.

Manuel was a prize. He would supply the
only thing I lacked in this most charming of
Spanish cities, — a boon companion with nothing to do. I made a bargain with him on the
spot, — so many pesetas per week, with three
meals a day, he to occupy the other side of the
table.

It was delightful to see him when the terms
were concluded. His face lighted up, and his
big brown eyes danced. Now he could hold up
his head. His father perhaps was right, but
what could he do ? Florita was so lovely ! Some

day I should see her; but not now; I would
not understand. His father by and by would
relent and send for him. Then he would take
my hand and place it in his father's and say,
"Here is the good painter who saved my life
and Florita's."

We ransacked Cordova from end to end:
into the mosque at twilight, sitting in the shadows of the forest of marble columns stretching
away on every side; up into the tower, where
the pigeons roost; across the old Roman bridge;
along the dusty highways on the outskirts of
the old city crowded with market people;
through the streets at night, listening to the
tinkling of guitars and watching the muffled
figures under the balconies, and the half-opened
lattices with the little hands waving handkerchiefs or dropping roses; everywhere and anywhere; in every nook and crack and cranny
of this once famous home of the hidalgo, the
cavalier, and the inamorata with the eyes of a
gazelle and the heart of fire.

Manuel loved it all. He loved, too, strange
to say, all things quaint and odd and old, and
in his enthusiasm had rummaged every sacristy
and priest's house for me in search of such
treasures. Indeed, there was hardly a pur-
chasable vestment or bit of embroidery in the

city that he had not bargained for, and my lodgings gave daily evidence of his success. One morning he came dancing in, bubbling over with delight, and swinging around his head a piece of brocade that would have made the mouth of an antiquary water. This he gravely informed me had once belonged to the figure of the good saint, the Santa Teresa, who had worn it for some hundreds of years, and who had parted with it the night before for ten pesetas. The sacristan who acted as her agent had replaced the exquisite relic with some new, cheap lace, explaining that it was the good saint's feast-day, and he was therefore especially desirous of presenting her properly to her devout admirers.

One subject, however, by common silent consent was tabooed, — the whereabouts of the sweetheart who had made him an exile. I knew that she was young, graceful as a doe, seductive as a houri, and beautiful beyond compare. I knew that she loved Manuel wildly, that he idolized her, and would starve rather than desert her. I knew also that she lived within a stone's throw of the café ; for Manuel would leave me at breakfast to kiss her good-morning, and at midday to kiss her again, and at sundown to kiss her once more good-night, and would return each time within ten minutes. I knew also, of course, that her name was Florita. All this the young fellow told me over and over again, with his face flushed and his eyes aflame; but I knew nothing more.

One night of each week was always Manuel's. Any part of any other night, or all of it, for that matter, was mine, and he was at my service for sightseeing or prowling; but Saturday was Florita's.

Except on festival nights, Saturday, of all nights in the week, is the gayest in all the Spanish cities. Then the cafés are in full blast, filled not only with the city people, but with the country folk who come to market on that day. These cafés have raised platforms, which are edged by a row of footlights, and hold half a dozen chairs seating as many male and female dancers. Here you see on gala nights the most bewitching of all the sights of Spain, — the Spanish dancers.

What music is to the Italian, dancing is to the Spaniard. Float along through any of the canals of Venice and listen: everybody is singing. The woman in the window of the wineshop over the way is humming an air from Trovatore. The idler on the quay joins in the melody, and in five minutes more the whole

71

waterway is ringing with its sublime harmony.
Turn out into the Grand Canal and so on into
the Lido. The boats from Chioggia, fish-laden,
are drifting up to the marble front of the Public
Garden, and the air is filled with the pathos of
some refrain a hundred years old. It is the language of the people ; they think, talk, vibrate
in music.

In Spain the outlet is through the toes, and
not only through the toes, but the feet, the
ankles, legs, up and through the spinal column,
out along the arms to the very finger-tips, every
nerve, tissue, muscle, and drop of blood in their
swinging, pulsating bodies tingling to the rhythm
of the dance. Under the influence of this magic
spell a man with one eye and a crooked leg,
head bound with a red handkerchief, jacket and
waistcoat off, will transform himself into an
embodiment of grace and expression. He will
give you whole columns of description with his
legs, avenge the forlorn heroine with the small
of his back, and deal death and destruction to
the villain with a twist of his head. It is the
condensation of the opera, the drama, the pan-
tomime, and the story-teller. Pictures, har-
monies, books, the platform, and the footlights
have their own well-worn roads to your brain ;

this language of the toes ploughs a furrow of its own.

On this particular Saturday night Manuel had taken himself off as usual, and I was left to follow my own free will alone. So I strolled into the garden of the mosque, sat me down on one of the stone seats under the orange-trees, and watched the women fill their water-jars at the old Moorish well, listening meanwhile to the chatter of their gossip. When it grew quite dark, I passed out through the Puerta del Perdon, turned to the right, and wandered on aimlessly down a narrow street leading to the river. Soon I heard the click of castanets and the thrum of guitars. There was a dance somewhere. Pushing aside a swinging door, I entered a small café.

The room was low-ceiled, apparently without windows, and the air stifling. The customary stage occupied one corner of the interior, which was crowded to the very walls with water-carriers, cargadors, gypsies, hucksters, and the young bloods of the town. They were cheering wildly a black-eyed señorita who had just finished her dance, and who was again at the footlights bowing her acknowledgments. She made a pretty picture in her short yellow skirts trimmed with black, her high comb, and her

lace mantilla, her bare arms waving gracefully.
I found a seat near the door, called for a bottle
of San Vicente, and lighted a cigarette. At the
adjoining table sat a group of young fellows
drinking aguardiente. It is a villanous liquor,
and more than a thimbleful sets a man's brain on
fire. They were measuring theirs in tumblers.
When at a second recall the girl again refused
to dance, the manager explaining that she was
very tired, the young caballeros began pound-
ing the table with their glasses, shouting out
in angry tones, " La señorita ! la señorita ! "
When for the third time the young girl advanced
to the platform's edge and bowed her regrets,
one of the group sprang forward, leaped upon
a table, and with an oath dashed the contents
of his glass over her bare shoulders. A frightened shriek cut the air, and the next instant a
heavy carafe filled with wine grazed my head,
struck the ruffian full in the face, and tumbled
him headlong to the floor.

Instantly the place was in an uproar. Half
a dozen men, one waving an ugly knife, sprang
past me, made a rush for the table in my rear,
and threw themselves upon a young fellow who
had thrown the carafe, and who stood with his
back to me, swinging its mate over his head like
a flail. Then came a crash, another Spaniard

74

sprawled on the floor, and a flying figure dashed
by and bounded over the footlights. As he
plunged through the curtain in the rear I caught
sight of his face. It was Manuel!

Grasping the situation, I sprang through the
door and reached the sidewalk just as the police
forced their way past me into the scattering
throng. A few sharp orders, a crash of breaking glass, a rattling of carbines on the floor, and
the tumult was over.

Humiliated at Manuel's deception, and yet
anxious for his safety, I hid myself in the shadow
near a street lamp, with my eye on the swinging door, and waited. The first man thrust out
was the ruffian who had emptied his glass over
the dancer. His arms were pinioned behind his
back, his head still bloody from the effects of
Manuel's carafe. Then came a villainous-look-
ing cut-throat with a gash across his cheek,
followed by three others, one of whom was the
manager.

The mob surrounded the group, the prison-
ers in front. I crouched close until they disappeared in a body up the street, then crossed
over, and swung back the door. The place was
empty. A man in his shirt-sleeves was putting
out the lights.

"There has been a row?" I said.

"Unquestionably."

"And some arrests ?"

"Yes, señor."

"Did they get them all ?"

"All but one."

"Where is he ?"

The man stopped, grinned the width of his face, and, thrusting up his thumb, waved it meaningly over his left shoulder.

Manuel had escaped !

For half the night I brooded over the unfaithfulness of human nature. Here was my hero telling lies to me about his Florita, spending his Saturday nights in a low café engaged in vulgar brawls, and all over a dancer. I began to consider and doubt. Was there any such fair creature at all as Florita ? Was there any implacable father ? Had Manuel ever been a student ? Was it not all a prearranged scheme to bleed me day by day and, awaiting a chance, rob me, or worse ? A man who could escape unhurt, surrounded as he had been, was no ordinary man. Perhaps he was simply a decoy for one of the numerous bands of brigands still infesting the mountains ; and I remembered with a shudder the story about the forefinger of the Englishman forwarded to his friends in a paper box as a sort of sight draft on his entire bank

76

account. I began to bless myself that mere accident had warned me in time. I would pick up no more impecunious tramps, with my heart and pocketbook wide open.

When the day broke, and the cheery sun that Manuel always loved streamed in my windows, the situation seemed to improve. I thought of his open, honest face, of his extreme kindness and gratitude, of the many delightful hours we had spent together. Perhaps, after all, it was not Manuel. I saw his face only for a moment, and these Spaniards are so much alike, all so dark and swarthy. He would surely come in an hour, and we would have our coffee together. I dragged a chair out on the balcony and sat down, watching anxiously the turn of the street where I had so often caught sight of him waving his hand.

At eight o'clock I gave him up. It was true; the face was Manuel's, and he dared not show himself now for fear of arrest. Then a new thought cheered me. Perhaps he was waiting at the café, or, it being Sunday, was late, and I would meet him on the way. How could I have misjudged him so? Filled with these thoughts I ran downstairs into the sunlight and stopped at the corner near the church, scanning the street up and down. There was no one I knew except the old bareheaded beggar with the withered arm. Manuel often gave him alms. He bowed as I passed, stood up, and put on his hat.

Near the café, at the bottom of the hill, stands a half-ruined archway. It can be reached by two streets running parallel and within a stone's-throw of each other. As I passed under this arch, the beggar, to my astonishment, started up as if from the ground. He had followed me.

"You are the painter, señor ?"

"Yes."

" And Manuel's friend ?"

" Of course ; where is he ?"

He glanced cautiously about, drew me under the shadow of the wall, and took a scrap of paper from inside the band of his hat.

It bore this inscription : —

"I am in trouble ; follow the beggar."

The old man looked at me fixedly, turned sharply, and retraced his steps through the arch. My decision was instantaneous ; I would find Manuel at all hazards.

The way led across the plaza of the bull-ring, through the fruit-market, up the hill past the little mosque, — now the church of Santa Maria, the one with the red marble altar, — and so on out into the suburbs of the city, the beggar keeping straight ahead and never looking behind. At the end of a narrow lane dividing two rows of old Moorish houses the mendicant tarried long enough for me to come quite near, glanced at me meaningly, and then disappeared in a crack in the wall. I followed, and found myself in a square patio, overgrown with weeds, half choked by the ruins of a fountain, and surrounded by a balcony supported by marble columns. This balcony was reached by a stone staircase. The beggar crossed the overgrown tangle, mounted the steps, swung back a heavy green door with Moorish hinges, and waited for me to pass in.

I drew back. The folly, if not the danger, of the whole proceeding began to dawn upon me.

"I will go no farther. Where is the man who sent you?"

The beggar placed his fingers to his lips and pointed behind him.

At the same instant a blind opened cautiously on the floor above, and Manuel's face, pale as a ghost, peered through the slats. The beggar entered, closed the heavy door carefully, felt his way along a dark corridor, and knocked twice. A shrivelled old woman with a bent back thrust out her head, mumbled something to the beggar, and led me to an opening in the opposite wall. Manuel sprang out and seized my hand.

"I knew you would come. Oh, such a scrape ! The police searched for us half the night. But for old Bonta, the beggar here, and his wife, we would have been caught. It would kill my father if anything should happen now. See, here is his letter saying we can come home ! Oh, I am so grateful to you ! You see it was this way. It was Florita's night, and I " —

My heart turned sick within me. Florita's night ! If the poor girl only knew !

" Don't say another word, Manuel ; you are in a scrape, and I will help you out, but don't lie about it to me of all men. If you love the dancer, all right. Breaking a carafe over a fellow's head in a café, and all for a pair of ankles, may be " —

" Lie to you, señor ! " said Manuel, flushing angrily, and with a certain dignity I had never seen in him before; " I could never lie to you. You do not know."

" I do know."

" Then Bonta has told you ? " and he looked towards the beggar.

" Bonta has not opened his lips. I saw it all with my own eyes, and you may thank your lucky stars that you were not sliced full of holes. What would Florita say ? "

"Florita ? Jesu, I see !" said Manuel, springing forward, pushing open the door, and calling
out : —

"Florita ! Are you there ? Come quick ! "

A hurried step in the adjoining room, and a
young girl came running in.

It was the dancer !

"What could I do, señor ? What would you
do if your own wife had been so insulted ? See
how lovely she is ! " And he kissed her on both
cheeks.

What would I have done ? What would you
have done, my friend, with that startled shriek
in your ears, her great eyes wet with tears, her
white arms held out to you ?

My hair is not quite so brown as it was, and
the blood no longer surges through my veins.
I am cooler and calmer, and even phlegmatic ;
and yet had Florita been mine, I would have
broken a carafe over every head in Cordova.

While he was calming her fears, kissing her
cheeks, and patting her hands, the whole story
came out. Day after day he had hoped that
his father would relent. One word from him,
and then I need never have known how the
dainty feet of his pretty young wife had helped
them both to live.

That night, a painter, with a pretty Spanish

cousin, and a servant carrying his coat and trap, occupied a first-class carriage for Toledo.

The painter left the train at the first station out of Cordova, shouldered his trap and coat himself, and took the night express back to his lonely lodgings. The servant and the señorita went on alone.

When the train reached Toledo, an old Spaniard with white head and mustache pushed his way through the crowd, took the servant in his arms, and kissed the pretty cousin on both cheeks.

Then a high-springed old coach swallowed them all up.

ANOTHER DOG

DO not tell me dogs cannot talk. I know
better. I saw it all myself. It was at
Sterzing, that most picturesque of all the Tyrolean villages on the Italian slope of the Bren-
ner, with its long, single street, zigzagged like
a straggling path in the snow, — perhaps it was
laid out in that way, — and its little open
square, with shrine and rude stone fountain,
surrounded by women in short skirts and hob-
nailed shoes, dipping their buckets. On both
sides of this street ran queer arcades sheltering
shops, their doorways piled with cheap stuffs,
fruit, farm implements, and the like, and at the
far end — it was almost the last house in the
town — stood the old inn, where you breakfast. Such an old, old inn! with swinging sign
framed by fantastic ironwork, and decorated
with overflows of foaming ale in green mugs,
crossed clay pipes, and little round dabs of yel-
low-brown cakes. There was a great archway,
too, wide and high, with enormous, barn-like
doors fronting on this straggling, zigzag, sabot-

83

trodden street. Under this a cobblestone pavement led to the door of the coffee-room and out
to the stable beyond. These barn-like doors
keep out the driving snows and the whirls of
sleet and rain, and are slammed to behind horse,
sleigh, and all, if not in the face, certainly in
the very teeth of the winter gale, while the
traveller disentangles his half-frozen legs at his
leisure, almost within sight of the blazing fire
of the coffee-room within.

Under this great archway, then, against one
of these doors, his big paws just inside the
shadow line, — for it was not winter, but a
brilliant summer morning, the grass all dusted
with powdered diamonds, the sky a turquoise,
the air a joy, — under this archway, I say, sat
a big St. Bernard dog, squat on his haunches,
his head well up, like a grenadier on guard.
His eyes commanded the approaches down the
road, up the road, and across the street; taking
in the passing pedler with the tinware, and
the girl with a basket strapped to her back, her
fingers knitting for dear life, not to mention so
unimportant an object as myself swinging down
the road, my iron-shod alpenstock hammering
the cobbles.

He made no objection to my entering, neither
did he receive me with any show of welcome.

ANOTHER DOG

There was no bounding forward, no wagging of the tail, no aimless walking around for a moment, and settling down in another spot; nor was there any sudden growl or forbidding look in the eye. None of these things occurred to him, for none of these things was part of his duty. The landlord would do the welcoming, the blue-shirted porter take my knapsack and show me the way to the coffee-room. His business was to sit still and guard that archway. Paying guests, and those known to the family, — yes! But stray mountain goats, chickens, inquisitive, pushing pedlers, pigs, and wandering dogs, — well, he would look out for these.

While the cutlets and coffee were being fried and boiled, I dragged a chair across the road and tilted it back out of the sun against the wall of a house. I, too, commanded a view down past the blacksmith shop, where they were heating a huge iron tire to clap on the hind wheel of a diligence, and up the street as far as the little square where the women were still clattering about on the cobbles, their buckets on their shoulders. This is how I happened to be watching the dog.

The more I looked at him, the more strongly did his personality impress me. The exceeding

85

gravity of his demeanor ! The dignified atti-
tude ! The quiet, silent reserve ! The way he
looked at you from under his eyebrows, not
eagerly, nor furtively, but with a self-possessed,
competent air, quite like a captain of a Cunarder
scanning a horizon from the bridge, or a French
gendarme watching the shifting crowds from
one of the little stone circles anchored out in
the rush of the boulevards, — a look of author-
ity backed by a sense of unlimited power.
Then, too, there was such a dignified cut to his
hairy chops as they drooped over his teeth beneath his black, stubby nose. His ears rose
and fell easily, without undue haste or excite-
ment when the sound of horses' hoofs put him
on his guard, or a goat wandered too near. Yet
one could see that he was not a meddlesome
dog, nor a snarler, no running out and giving
tongue at each passing object, not that kind of
a dog at all ! He was just a plain, substantial,
well - mannered, dignified, self-respecting St.
Bernard dog, who knew his place and kept it,
who knew his duty and did it, and who would
no more chase a cat than he would bite your
legs in the dark. Put a cap with a gold band
on his head, and he would really have made
an ideal concierge. Even without the band, he
concentrated in his person all the superiority,

the repose and exasperating reticence of that necessary concomitant of Continental hotel life.

Suddenly I noticed a more eager expression on his face. One ear was unfurled, like a flag, and almost run to the masthead ; the head was turned quickly down the road. A sound of wheels was heard below the shop. His dogship straightened himself and stood on four legs, his tail wagging slowly.

Another dog was coming.

A great Danish hound, with white eyes, black-and-tan ears, and tail as long and smooth as a policeman's night-club, — one of those sleek and shining dogs with powerful chest and knotted legs, a little bowed in front, black lips, and dazzling, fang-like teeth. He was spattered with brown spots, and sported a single white foot. Altogether, he was a dog of quality, of ancestry, of a certain position in his own land, — one who had clearly followed his master's mountain wagon to-day as much for love of adventure as anything else. A dog of parts, too, who could, perhaps, hunt the wild boar, or give chase to the agile deer. He was certainly not an inn dog. He was rather a palace dog, a chateau or a shooting-box dog, who, in his off moments, trotted behind hunting carts filled with

87

guns, sportsmen in knee-breeches, or in front of landaus when my lady went an airing.

And with all this, and quite naturally, he was a dog of breeding, who, while he insisted on his own rights, respected those of others. I saw this before he had spoken ten words to the concierge, — the St. Bernard dog, I mean. For he did talk to him, and the conversation was just as plain to me, tilted back against the wall, out of the sun, waiting for my cutlets and coffee, as if I had been a dog myself, and understood each word of it.

First, he walked up sideways, his tail wagging and straight out, like a patent towel-rack. Then he walked round the concierge, who followed his movements with becoming interest, wagging his own tail, straightening his forelegs, and sidling around him kindly, as befitted the stranger's rank and quality, but with a certain dog - independence of manner, preserving his own dignities while courteously passing the time of day, and intimating, by certain twists of his tail, that he felt quite sure his excellency would like the air and scenery the farther he got up the pass, — all strange dogs did.

During this interchange of canine civilities, the landlord was helping out the two men, the companions of the dog. One was round and pudgy, the other lank and scrawny. Both were in knickerbockers, with green hats decorated with cock feathers and edelweiss. The blue-shirted porter carried in the bags and alpenstocks, closing the coffee-room door behind them.

Suddenly the strange dog, who had been beguiled by the courteous manner of the concierge, realized that his master had disappeared. The man had been hungry, no doubt, and half blinded by the glare of the sun. After the manner of his kind, he had dived into this shelter without a word to the dumb beast who had tramped behind his wheels, swallowing the dust his horses kicked up.

When the strange dog realized this, — I saw the instant the idea entered his mind, as I caught the sudden toss of the head, — he glanced quickly about with that uneasy, anxious look that comes into the face of a dog when he discovers that he is adrift in a strange place without his master. What other face is so utterly miserable, and what eyes so pleading, the tears just under the lids, as the lost dog's ?

Then it was beautiful to see the St. Bernard. With a sudden twist of the head he reassured the strange dog, — telling him, as plainly as

89

could be, not to worry, the gentlemen were only inside, and would be out after breakfast. There was no mistaking what he said. It was done with a peculiar curving of the neck, a re-assuring wag of the tail, a glance toward the coffee-room, and a few frolicsome, kittenish jumps, these last plainly indicating that as for himself the occasion was one of great hilarity, with absolutely no cause in it for anxiety. Then, if you could have seen that anxious look fade away from the face of the strange dog, the responsive, reciprocal wag of the night-club of a tail. If you could have caught the sudden peace that came into his eyes, and have seen him as he followed the concierge to the door-way, dropping his ears, and throwing himself beside him, looking up into his face, his tongue out, panting after the habit of his race, the white saliva dropping upon his paws.

Then followed a long talk, conducted in side glances, and punctuated with the quiet laughs of more slappings of tails on the cobbles, as the concierge listened to the adventures of the stranger, or matched them with funny experiences of his own.

Here a whistle from the coffee-room window startled them. Even so rude a being as a man is sometimes mindful of his dog. In an instant

both concierge and stranger were on their feet,
the concierge ready for whatever would turn
up, the stranger trying to locate the sound and
his master. Another whistle, and he was off,
bounding down the road, looking wistfully at
the windows, and rushing back bewildered.
Suddenly it came to him that the short cut to
his master lay through the archway.

Just here there was a change in the manner
of the concierge. It was not gruff, nor savage,
nor severe, — it was only firm and decided.
With his tail still wagging, showing his kindness and willingness to oblige, but with spine
rigid and hair bristling, he explained clearly and
succinctly to that strange dog how absolutely
impossible it would be for him to permit his
crossing the archway. Up went the spine of
the stranger, and out went his tail like a bar of
steel, the feet braced, and the whole body taut
as standing rigging. But the concierge kept on
wagging his tail, though his hair still bristled,
— saying as plainly as he could : —

"My dear sir, do not blame me. I assure
you that nothing in the world would give me
more pleasure than to throw the whole house
open to you ; but consider for a moment. My
master puts me here to see that nobody enters
the inn but those whom he wishes to see, and

that all other live-stock, especially dogs, shall
on no account be admitted." (This with head
bent on one side and neck arched.) "Now,
while I have the most distinguished consideration for your dogship " (tail wagging violently),
" and would gladly oblige you, you must see
that my honor is at stake " (spine more rigid),
" and I feel assured that under the circumstances you will not press a request " (low
growl) "which you must know would be impossible for me to grant."

And the strange dog, gentleman as he was,
expressed himself as entirely satisfied with the
very free and generous explanation. With tail
wagging more violently than ever, he assured
the concierge that he understood his position
exactly. Then wheeling suddenly, he bounded
down the road. Though convinced, he was still
anxious.

Then the concierge gravely settled himself
once more on his haunches in his customary
place, his eyes commanding the view up and
down and across the road, where I sat still
tilted back in my chair waiting for my cutlets,
his whole body at rest, his face expressive of
that quiet content which comes from a sense of
duties performed and honor untarnished.

But the stranger had duties, too ; he must

answer the whistle, and find his master. His search down the road being fruitless, he rushed back to the concierge, looking up into his face, his eyes restless and anxious.

"If it were inconsistent with his honor to permit him to cross the threshold, was there any other way he could get into the coffee-room ? " This last with a low whine of uneasiness, and a toss of head.

"Yes, certainly," jumping to his feet, "why had he not mentioned it before ? It would give him very great pleasure to show him the way to the side entrance." And the St. Bernard, everything wagging now, walked with the stranger to the corner, stopping stock still to point with his nose to the closed door.

Then the stranger bounded down with a scurry and plunge, nervously edging up to the door, wagging his tail, and with a low, anxious whine springing one side and another, his paws now on the sill, his nose at the crack, until the door was finally opened, and he dashed inside.

What happened in the coffee-room I do not know, for I could not see. I am willing, however, to wager that a dog of his loyalty, dignity, and sense of duty did just what a dog of quality would do. No awkward springing at his master's chest with his dusty paws leaving marks

on his vest front; no rushing around chairs
and tables in mad joy at being let in, alarming
waitresses and children. Only a low whine
and gurgle of delight, a rubbing of his cold nose
against his master's hand, a low, earnest look
up into his face, so frank, so trustful, a look
that carried no reproach for being shut out, and
only gratitude for being let in.

A moment more, and he was outside again,
head in air, looking for his friend. Then a dash,
and he was around by the archway, licking the
concierge in the face, biting his neck, rubbing
his nose under his fore legs, saying over and
over again how deeply he thanked him, — how
glad and proud he was of his acquaintance, and
how delighted he would be if he came down
to Vienna, or Milan, or wherever he did come
from, so that he might return his courtesies in
some way, and make his stay pleasant.

Just here the landlord called out that the
cutlets and coffee were ready, and, man like,
I went in to breakfast.

LA CANAL DE LA VIGA

IT begins at the great lakes, away up in the
country, among the flowers and market
gardens, winds in and out of the low hills and
hollows, stopping at the various Aztec towns
with the unpronounceable names. Then it takes
a turn into the little holiday village of Santa
Anita, where the flower-crowned peons dance
feast-days and Sundays, waters the edges of
the *chinampas*, — the floating gardens of the
ancients overgrown with weeds and anchored
by neglect, — flows past the almost deserted
paseo de la Viga, holding half-way its length
the dilapidated bust of Guatimotzin, and so on
down to the City of Mexico.

All kinds of water craft loaded with all kinds
of merchandise float up and down its windings :
wood boats ; market boats ; flower boats ; canoes filled with Indians ; flat-bottomed barges
roofed over with a rude awning amidships, —
barbaric gondolas, crowded with merrymakers
thrumming guitars and clicking castanets, — a
steady stream of life, with the current towards
the city.

95

Here it is swallowed up like many another
fresh young life joyous from the green fields.
Here the city pounces upon it and defiles it.
Here every bit of stray refuse, every scrap of
offal, all the filth, all the dirt, all the scrapings
and castaways of the great city are thrust into
its pure waters. Even the narrow little bridges
take a hand in the villany; crowding and jos-
tling as if bent on choking it up forever.

Soon it reaches the slums, the very dregs of
its pollution; the stables; the dyehouses and
the sewers; the slaughter-houses, where the
brown-backed peons, naked to the waist, lean
over rotting logs cleansing the reeking hides
fresh from the shambles. Every indignity is
heaped upon it, every touch befouls it.

Still it struggles on, cringing like an outcast,
slinking under the bridges, crouching through
dark waterways, edging along rotting embank-
ments, buoyed up and strengthened by the
thought of the bright pure waters of Lake Tex-
coco glistening in the sunlight a few miles
away.

You follow down, in and out, crossing and
recrossing the little bridges, hugging the shadows of the tall pink and yellow washed buildings, — their balconies trellised with flowers
and hooded with awnings, — until you come to

where the water widens out, washing a broad
flight of stone steps that lead up to four great
columns supporting the entablature and roof of
an imposing structure quite classic in its design.
This is the Mercado del Pulquerria.

Cross the little bridge above, pick your way
through the crowds of venders in the street,
push through the babel of buyers and sellers on
the floor of the market, and walk out into the
blinding sunlight on the very same stone steps
you saw from across the canal. A sight greets
you that exists only in one spot the world over.

Beneath, in a solid pack, their sides touching, floats a great fleet of canoes loaded to the
water's edge with masses of flowers, heaps of
vegetables, piles upon piles of fruit : — one solid
carpet of blue larkspur, bright marigolds and
carnations, poppies, roses, radishes, lettuce,
tomatoes, melons, grapes, and figs.

You forget the ninety and nine smells, the
seething, bubbling hides, the ooze and slime of
the sodden logs, and revel only in the sunlight,
the palms waving over the low walls, the blazing, dazzling white of the great building opposite, the deep blue of the sky overhead, and the
superb carpet of color dotted with figures beneath.

Stand behind one of the great pillars within a

97

few feet of the nearest boat. Its bow is a mass of blue larkspur and ragged sailors. Amidships is a great square of carnations, intermingled with every variety of reds and yellows. In the stern stands a peon girl, her head covered by a wide-peaked sombrero of yellow straw, throwing the richly colored face in shadow.

The sunlight falls on her bare arms and back, and glistens on the white chemise, half concealing the full outlines of her rounded figure. About her hips is folded a square, blue cotton blanket, girded by a red sash. In her ears are large silver hoops. An armlet of copper binds one arm near the shoulder.

She stands erect, steadying herself, — one hand on the oar, which in turn steadies the boat, the other filled with fruit and flowers. These she lifts up to the clamoring crowd, tossing them now a bunch of radishes, now a cluster of carnations in exchange for their copper coins, which she catches dexterously in mid-air.

If you think grace died with the Greeks, watch this girl for a moment. She is barely sixteen ; her eyes are dark and luminous ; her hair a purple black, tied in two great braids down her back ; her teeth white as milk ; her neck, arms, and bust exquisitely modelled ; her

fingers small and tapering, and her feet tiny
enough to dance on Persian carpets. She has a
skin that is not the red of the Indian, nor brown,
nor quadroon ; it is light though transparent
copper.

Every movement is grace itself. That she
comes of an indolent race only adds to her
beauty. Minutes at a time she keeps perfectly
still, even to her eyelids. Then she shifts the
oar, throws her weight on the other hip, her
beautiful bare arms fall to her side, and she is
more entrancing than ever. She is absolutely
unconscious of your admiration. She has but
one thought in life, — to sell her cargo before
the hot sun shall shrivel it up.

Suddenly, above the din of the traffic, you
hear a sharp cry. The girl starts forward, drops
the oar, and falls on her knees in the boat, among
the greens and flowers. When she rises she has
her little bare, bronze baby in her arms.

At the same instant, from underneath, there
crawls out a shaggy-headed peon rubbing his
eyes. He has been sound asleep. Long before
the gray dawn, and many weary miles from
here, he had poled the canoe alone ; past the
sleeping villages and the *chinampas,* while the
mother and child rested.

The crowd thins out. One by one the boats

99

drop off, and drift up or down. Soon the bronze goddess and her baby and her shaggy-headed husband float by with an empty boat.

You look after them long and musingly, until they are lost in the throng. Then, somehow, you feel a slight pain, as of a personal loss. The place is different, the charm has fled.

You begin to note the foul water strewn with waste leaves, decayed fruit, and the offal of the market. You become aware of the stench and the reeking filth. The white wall glows like a furnace, — the sky is molten brass, — the palms hang limp. You turn in disgust and enter the stifling market, where barelegged peons are drenching the foul stone flags with fouler water from the canal, and so on through and out into the narrow street, dodging under the awnings, and skirting close to the strip of a black shadow stenciled on the sidewalk.

Soon you reach your garden, and the cool of your quiet siesta.

Over your coffee you have but one memory, — the grand figure of that daughter of Montezuma, radiant in the sunlight, her hands filled with flowers.

A KNIGHT OF THE LEGION OF HONOR

IT was in the smoking-room of a Cunarder two days out. The evening had been spent in telling stories, the fresh-air passengers crowding the doorways to listen, the habitual loungers and card-players abandoning their books and games.

When my turn came, — mine was a story of Venice, a story of the old palace of the Barbarozzi, — I noticed in one corner of the room a man seated alone wrapped in a light shawl, who had listened intently as he smoked, but who took no part in the general talk. He attracted my attention from his likeness to my friend Vereschagin the painter; his broad, white forehead, finely wrought features, clear, honest, penetrating eye, flowing mustache and beard streaked with gray, — all strongly suggestive of that distinguished Russian. I love Vereschagin, and so, unconsciously, and by mental association, perhaps, I was drawn to this stranger. Seeing my eye fixed constantly upon him, he threw off his shawl, and crossed the room.

" Pardon me, but your story about the Barbarozzi brought to my mind so many delightful recollections that I cannot help thanking you. I know that old palace, — knew it thirty years ago, — and I know that cortile, and although I have not had the good fortune to run across either your gondolier, Espero, or his sweetheart, Mariana, I have known a dozen others as romantic and delightful. The air is stifling here. Shall we have our coffee outside on the deck ? "

When we were seated, he continued, " And so you are going to Venice to paint ? "

" Yes ; and you ? "

" Me ? Oh, to the Engadine to rest. American life is so exhausting that I must have these three months of quiet to make the other nine possible."

The talk drifted into the many curious adventures befalling a man in his journeyings up and down the world, most of them suggested by the queer stories of the night. When coffee had been served, he lighted another cigar, held the match until it burned itself out, — the yellow flame lighting up his handsome face, — looked out over the broad expanse of tranquil sea, with its great highway of silver leading up to the full moon dominating the night, and said as if in deep thought : —

"And so you are going to Venice ? " Then, after a long pause : " Will you mind if I tell you of an adventure of my own, — one still most vivid in my memory ? It happened near there many years ago." He picked up his shawl, pushed our chairs close to the overhanging life-boat, and continued : —

"I had begun my professional career, and had gone abroad to study the hospital system in Europe. The revolution in Poland — the re-volt of '62 — had made travelling in northern Europe uncomfortable, if not dangerous, for foreigners, even with the most authentic of passports, and so I had spent the summer in Italy. One morning early in the autumn, I bade good-by to my gondolier at the water-steps of the railroad station, and bought a ticket for Vienna. An important letter required my immediate presence in Berlin.

"On entering the train I found the carriage occupied by two persons : a lady, richly dressed, but in deep mourning and heavily veiled ; and a man, dark and smooth-faced, wearing a high silk hat. Raising my cap, I placed my umbrella and smaller traps under the seat, and hung my bundle of travelling shawls in the rack overhead.

The lady returned my salutation gravely, lifting her veil and making room for my bundles. The dark man's only response was a formal touching of his hat-brim with his forefinger.

"The lady interested me instantly. She was perhaps twenty-five years of age, graceful, and of distinguished bearing. Her hair was jet-black, brushed straight back from her temples, her complexion a rich olive, her teeth pure white. Her lashes were long, and opened and shut with a slow, fan-like movement, shading a pair of deep blue eyes, which shone with that peculiar light only seen when quick tears lie hidden under half-closed lids. Her figure was rounded and full, and her hands exquisitely modelled. Her dress, while of the richest material, was perfectly plain, with a broad white collar and cuffs like those of a nun. She wore no jewels of any kind. I judged her to be a woman of some distinction, — an Italian or Hungarian, perhaps.

"When the train started, the dark man, who had remained standing, touched his hat to me, raised it to the lady, and disappeared. Her only acknowledgment was a slight inclination of the head. A polite stranger, no doubt, I thought, who prefers the smoker. When the train stopped for luncheon, I noticed that the lady did not leave the carriage, and on my return I found her still seated, looking listlessly out of the window, her head upon her hand.

"'Pardon me, madame,' I said in French, 'but unless you travel some distance this is the last station where you can get anything to eat.'

"She started, and looked about helplessly. 'I am not hungry. I cannot eat — but I suppose I should.'

"'Permit me;' and I sprang from the carriage, and caught a waiter with a tray before the guard reclosed the doors. She drank the coffee, tasted the fruit, thanking me in a low, sweet voice, and said : —

"'You are very considerate. It will help me to bear my journey. I am very tired and weaker than I thought ; for I have not slept for many nights.'

"I expressed my sympathy, and ended by telling her I hoped we could keep the carriage to ourselves ; she might then sleep undisturbed. She looked at me fixedly, a curious startled expression crossing her face, but made no reply.

"Almost every man is drawn, I think, to a sad or tired woman. There is a look about the eyes that makes an instantaneous draft on the sympathies. So, when these slight confidences of my companion confirmed my misgivings as to her own weariness, I at once began diverting her as best I could with some account of my summer's experience in Venice, and with such of my plans for the future as at the moment filled my mind. I was younger then, — perhaps only a year or two her senior, — and you know one is not given to much secrecy at twenty-six: certainly not with a gentle lady whose good-will you are trying to gain, and whose sorrowful face, as I have said, enlists your sympathy at sight. Then, to establish some sort of footing for myself, I drifted into an account of my own home life; telling her of my mother and sisters, of the social customs of our country, of the freedom given the women, — so different from what I had seen abroad, — of their perfect safety everywhere.

"We had been talking in this vein some time, she listening quietly until something I said reacted in a slight curl of her lips, — more incredulous than contemptuous, perhaps, but significant all the same; for, lifting her eyes, she answered slowly and meaningly: —

"'It must be a paradise for women. I am glad to believe that there is one corner of the earth where they are treated with respect. My own experiences have been so different that I have begun to believe that none of us are safe

after we leave our cradles.' Then, as if suddenly realizing the inference, the color mount-
ing to her cheeks, she added : ' But please do
not misunderstand me. I am quite willing to
accept your statement ; for I never met an
American before.'

" As we neared the foothills the air grew
colder. She instinctively drew her cloak the
closer, settling herself in one corner and closing
her eyes wearily. I offered my rug, insisting
that she was not properly clad for a journey
over the mountains at night. She refused gently
but firmly, and closed her eyes again, resting
her head against the dividing cushion. For a
moment I watched her ; then arose from my
seat, and, pulling down my bundle of shawls,
begged that I might spread my heaviest rug
over her lap. An angry color mounted to her
cheeks. She turned upon me, and was about
to refuse indignantly, when I interrupted : —

" ' Please allow me ; don't you know you
cannot sleep if you are cold ? Let me put this
wrap about you. I have two.'

" With the unrolling, the leather tablet of the
shawl-strap, bearing my name, fell in her lap.

" ' Your name is Bosk,' she said, with a
quick start, ' and you an American ?'

" ' Yes ; why not ?'

" ' My maiden name is Boski,' she replied, looking at me in astonishment, 'and I am a Pole.'

" Here were two mysteries solved. She was married, and neither Italian nor Slav.

" ' And your ancestry ?' she continued with increased animation. ' Are you of Polish blood? You know our name is a great name in Poland. Your grandfather, of course, was a Pole.' Then, with deep interest, ' What are your armorial bearings ?'

" I answered that I had never heard that my grandfather was a Pole. It was quite possible, though, that we might be of Polish descent, for my father had once told me of an ancestor, an old colonel, who fell at Austerlitz. As to the armorial bearings, we Americans never cared for such things. The only thing I could remember was a certain seal which my father used to wear, and with which he sealed his letters. The tradition in the family was that it belonged to this old colonel. My sister used it sometimes. I had a letter from her in my pocket.

" She examined the indented wax on the envelope, opened her cloak quickly, and took from the bag at her side a seal mounted in jewels, bearing a crest and coat of arms.

" ' See how slight the difference. The quar-

terings are almost the same, and the crest and
motto identical. This side is mine, the other is
my husband's. How very, very strange ! And
yet you are an American ?'

" ' And your husband's crest?' I asked. ' Is
he also a Pole ?'

" ' Yes ; I married a Pole,' with a slight
trace of haughtiness, even resentment, at the
inquiry.

" ' And his name, madame ? Chance has
given you mine — a fair exchange is never a
robbery.'

" She drew herself up, and said quickly, and
with a certain bearing I had not noticed before : —

" ' Not now ; it makes no difference.'

" Then, as if uncertain of the effect of her
refusal, and with a willingness to be gracious,
she added : —

" ' In a few minutes — at ten o'clock — we
reach Trieste. The train stops twenty minutes.
You were so kind about my luncheon ; I am
stronger now. Will you dine with me ?'

" I thanked her, and on arriving at Trieste
followed her to the door. As we alighted from
the carriage I noticed the same dark man standing by the steps, his fingers on his hat. During
the meal my companion seemed brighter and

less weary, more gracious and friendly, until I
called the waiter and counted out the florins on
his tray. Then she laid her hand quietly but
firmly upon my arm.

" 'Please do not — you distress me ; my
servant Polaff has paid for everything.'

"I looked up. The dark man was standing
behind her chair, his hat in his hand.

" I can hardly express to you my feelings as
these several discoveries revealed to me little
by little the conditions and character of my
travelling companion. Brought up myself under
a narrow home influence, with only a limited
knowledge of the world, I had never yet been
thrown in with a woman of her class. And yet
I cannot say that it was altogether the charm
of her person that moved me. It was more a
certain hopeless sort of sorrow that seemed to
envelop her, coupled with an indefinable distrust which I could not solve. Her reserve,
however, was impenetrable, and her guarded
silence on every subject bearing upon herself
so pronounced that I dared not break through
it. Yet, as she sat there in the carriage after
dinner, during the earlier hours of the night, she
and I the only occupants, her eyes heavy and
red for want of sleep, her beautiful hair bound
in a veil, the pallor of her skin intensified by

the sombre hues of her dress, I would have given anything in the world to have known her well enough to have comforted her, even by a word.

"As the night wore on, the situation became intolerable. Every now and then she would start from her seat, jostled awake by the roughness of the road, — this section had just been completed, — turn her face the other way, only to be awakened again.

"'You cannot sleep. May I make a pillow for your head of my other shawl? I do not need it. My coat is warm enough.'

"'No; I am very comfortable.'

"'Forgive me, you are not. You are very uncomfortable, and it pains me to see you so weary. These dividing-irons make it impossible for you to lie down. Perhaps I can make a cushion for your head so that you will rest easier.'

"She looked at me coldly, her eyes riveted on mine.

"'You are very kind, but why do you care? You have never seen me before, and may never again.'

"'I care because you are a woman, alone and unprotected. I care most because you are suffering. Will you let me help you?'

III

"She bent her head, and seemed wrapped in thought. Then straightening up, as if her mind had suddenly resolved : —

"'No; leave me alone. I will sleep soon. Men never really care for a woman when she suffers.' She turned her face to the window.

"'I pity you, then, from the bottom of my heart,' I replied, nettled at her remark. 'There is not a man the length and breadth of my land who would not feel for you now as I do, and there is not a woman who would misunderstand him.'

"She raised her head, and in a softened voice, like a sorrowing child's, it was so pathetic, said : 'Please forgive me. I had no right to speak so. I shall be very grateful to you if you can help me. I am so tired !'

"I folded the shawl, arranged the rug over her knees, and took the seat beside her. She thanked me, laid her cheek upon the impromptu pillow, and closed her eyes. The train sped on, the carriage swaying as we rounded the curves, the jolting increasing as we neared the great tunnel. Settling myself in my seat, I drew my travelling-cap well down, so that its shadow from the overhead light would conceal my eyes, and watched her unobserved. For half an hour I followed every line in her face, with its delicate nostrils, finely cut nose, white temples with their blue veins, and the beautiful hair glistening in the half-shaded light, the long lashes resting, tired out, upon her cheek. Soon I noticed at irregular intervals a nervous twitching pass over her face ; the brow would knit and relax wearily, the mouth droop. These indications of extreme exhaustion occurred constantly, and alarmed me. Unchecked, they would result in an alarming form of nervous prostration. A sudden lurch dislodged the pillow.

"'Have you slept ? ' I asked.

"'I do not know. A little, I think. The car shakes so.'

"'My dear lady,' I said, laying my hand on hers, — she started, but did not move her own, — 'it is absolutely necessary that you sleep, and at once. What your nervous strain has been, I know not ; but my training tells me that it has been excessive, and still is. Its continuance is dangerous. This road gets rougher as the night passes. If you will rest your head upon my shoulder, I can hold you so that you will go to sleep.'

"Her face flushed, and she recovered her hand quickly.

"'You forget, sir, that' —

"'No, no ; I forget nothing. I remember

113

everything ; that I am a stranger, that you are
ill, that you are rapidly growing worse, that,
knowing as I do your condition, I cannot sit
here and not help you. It would be brutal.'

" Her lips quivered, and her eyes filled. ' I
believe you,' she said. Then, turning quickly
with an anxious look, ' But it will tire you.'

" ' No ; I have held my mother that way for
hours at a time.'

" She put out her hand, laid it gently on my
wrist, looked into my face long and steadily,
scanning every feature, as if reassuring herself,
then laid her cheek upon my shoulder, and fell
asleep.

" When the rising sun burst behind a mountain crag, and, at a turn in the road, fell full
upon her face, she awoke with a start, and
looked about bewildered. Then her mind cleared.

" ' How good you have been! You have not
moved all night so I might rest. I awoke once
frightened, but your hands were folded in your
lap.'

" With this her whole manner changed. All
the haughty reserve was gone ; all the cyni-
cism, the distrust, and suspicion. She became
as gentle and tender as an anxious mother,
begging me to go to sleep at once. She would

see that no one disturbed me. It was cruel that I was so exhausted.

"When the guard entered, she sent for her servant, and bade him watch out for a pot of coffee at the next station. ' To think monsieur had not slept all night ! ' When Polaff handed in the tray, she filled the cups herself, adding the sugar, and insisting that I should also drink part of her own, — one cup was not enough. Upon Polaff's return she sent for her dressing-case. She must make her toilet at once, and not disturb me. It would be several hours before we reached Vienna ; she felt sure I would sleep now.

"I watched her as she spread a dainty towel over the seat in front, and began her preparations, laying out the powder-boxes, brushes, and comb, the bottles of perfume, and the little knickknacks that make up the fittings of a gentlewoman's boudoir. It was almost with a show of enthusiasm that she picked up one of the bottles, and pointed out to me again the crest in relief upon its silver top, saying over and over again how glad she was to know that some of her own blood ran in my veins. She was sure now that I belonged to her father's people. When, at the next station, Polaff brought a basin of water, and I arose to leave

the car, she begged me to remain, — the toilet
was nothing ; it would be over in a minute.
Then she loosened her hair, letting it fall in
rich masses about her shoulders, and bathed her
face and hands, rearranging her veil, and adding a fresh bit of lace to her throat. I remember distinctly how profound an impression this
strange scene made upon my mind, so different
from any former experience of my life, — its
freedom from conventionality, the lack of all
false modesty, the absolute absence of any touch
of coquetry or conscious allurement.

"When it was all over, her beauty being all
the more pronounced now that the tired, nervous look had gone out of her face, she still
talked on, saying how much better and fresher
she felt, and how much more rested than the
night before. Suddenly her face saddened, and
for many minutes she kept silence, gazing
dreamily down into the abysses white with the
rush of Alpine torrents, or hidden in the early
morning fog. Then, finding that I would not
sleep, and with an expression as if she had
finally resolved upon some definite action, and
with a face in which every line showed the sin-
cerest confidence and trust, — as unexpected as
it was incomprehensible to me, — she said : —

" 'Last night you asked me for my name.

I would not tell you then. Now you shall know. I am the Countess de Rescka Smolenski. I live in Cracow. My husband died in Venice four days ago. I took him there because he was ill, — so ill that he was carried in Polaff's arms from the gondola to his bed. The Russian government permitted me to take him to Italy to die. One Pole the less is of very little consequence. A week ago this permit was revoked, and we were ordered to report at Cracow without delay. Why, I do not know, except perhaps to add another cruelty to the long list of wrongs the government has heaped upon my family. My husband lingered three days with the order spread out on the table beside him. The fourth day they laid him in Campo Santo. That night my maid fell ill. Yesterday morning a second peremptory order was handed me. I am now on my way home to obey.'

"Then followed in slow, measured sentences the story of her life : married at seventeen at her father's bidding to a man twice her age ; surrounded by a court the most dissolute in eastern Europe ; forced into a social environment that valued woman only as a chattel, and that ostracized or defamed every wife who, reverencing her womanhood, protested against its excesses. For five years past — ever since

117

her marriage — her husband's career had been one long, unending dissipation. At last, broken down by a life he had not the moral courage to resist, he had succumbed and taken to his bed ; thence, wavering between life and death, like a burnt-out candle flickering in its socket, he had been carried to Venice.

"'Do you wonder, now, that my faith is gone, my heart broken ? '

"We were nearing Vienna ; the stations were more frequent ; our own carriage began filling up. For an hour we rode side by side, silent, she gazing fixedly from the window, I half stunned by this glimpse of a life the pathos of which wrung my very heart. When we entered the station she roused herself, and said to me half pleadingly : —

"'I cannot bear to think I may never see you again. To-night I must stay in Vienna. Will you dine with me at my hotel ? I go to the Metropole. And you ? Where did you intend to go ? '

"'To the Metropole, also.'

"'Not when you left Venice ? '

"'Yes ; before I met you.'

"'There is a fate that controls us,' she said reverently. ' Come at seven.'

"When the hour arrived I sent my card to

her apartment, and was ushered into a small room with a curtain - closed door opening out into a larger salon, through which I caught glimpses of a table spread with glass and silver. Polaff, rigid and perpendicular, received me with a stiff, formal recognition. I do not think he quite understood, nor altogether liked his mistress's chance acquaintance. In a moment she entered from a door opposite, still in her black garments with the nun's cuffs and broad collar. Extending her hand graciously, she said : —

" ' You have slept since I left you this morning. I see it in your face. I am so glad. And I too. I have rested all day. It was so good of you to come.'

" There was no change in her manner ; the same frank, trustful look in her eyes, the same anxious concern about me. When dinner was announced she placed me beside her, Polaff standing behind her chair, and the other attendants serving.

" The talk drifted again into my own life, she interrupting with pointed questions, and making me repeat again and again the stories I told her of our humble home. She must learn them herself to tell them to her own people, she said. It was all so strange and new to her, so simple and so genuine! With the coffee she fell to talking of her own home, the despotism of Russia, the death of her father, the forcing of her brothers into the army. Still holding her cup in her hands, she began pacing up and down, her eyes on the floor (we were alone, Polaff having retired). Then stopping in front of me, and with an earnestness that startled me :

" ' Do not go to Berlin. Please come to Cracow with me. Think! I am alone, absolutely alone. My house is in order, and has been for months, expecting me every day. It is so terrible to go back ; come with me, please.'

" ' I must not, madame. I have promised my friends to be in Berlin in two days. I would, you know, sacrifice anything of my own to serve you.'

" ' And you will not ? ' and a sigh of disappointment escaped her.

" ' I cannot.'

" ' No ; I must not ask you. You are right. It is better that you keep your word.'

" She continued walking, gazing still on the floor. Then she moved to the mantel, and touched a bell. Instantly the curtains of the door divided, and Polaff stood before her.

" ' Bring me my jewel-case.'

" The man bowed gravely, looked at me furtively from the corner of his eye, and closed the curtains behind him. In a moment he returned, bearing a large, morocco-covered box, which he placed on the table. She pressed the spring, and the lid flew up, uncovering several velvet-lined trays filled with jewels that flashed under the lighted candles.

" 'You need not wait, Polaff. You can go to bed.'

" The man stepped back a pace, stood by the wall, fixed his eye upon his mistress, as if about to speak, looked at me curiously, then, bowing low, drew the curtains aside, and closed the door behind him.

" Another spring, and out came a great string of pearls, a necklace of sapphires, some rubies and emeralds. These she heaped up upon the white cloth beside her. Carefully examining the contents of the case, she drew from a lower tray a bracelet set with costly diamonds, a rare and beautiful ornament, and before I was aware of her intent had clasped it upon my wrist.

" 'I want you to wear this for me. You see it is large enough to go quite up the arm.'

" For a moment my astonishment was so great I could not speak. Then I loosened it and laid it in her hand again. She looked up, her eyes filling, her face expressive of the deepest pain.

" ' And you will not ? '

" ' I cannot, madame. In my country men do not accept such costly presents from women, and then we do not wear bracelets, as your men do here.'

" ' Then take this case, and choose for yourself.'

" I poured the contents of a small tray into my hand, and picked out a plain locket, almond-shaped, simply wrought, with an opening on one side for hair.

" ' Give me this with your hair.'

" She threw the bracelet into the case, and her eyes lighted up.

" ' Oh, I am so glad, so glad ! It was mine when I was a child, — my mother gave it to me. The dear little locket — yes, you shall always wear it.'

" Then rising from her seat, she took my hands in hers, and looking down into my face, said, her voice breaking : —

" ' It is eleven o'clock. Soon you must leave me. You cannot stay longer. I know that in a few hours I shall never see you again. Will you join me in my prayers before I go ? '

" A few minutes later she called to me. She was on her knees in the next room, two candles burning beside her, her rich dark hair loose

about her shoulders, an open breviary bound
with silver in her hands. I can see her now,
with her eyes closed, her lips moving noiselessly, her great lashes wet with tears, and
that Madonna-like look as she motioned me to
kneel. For several minutes she prayed thus,
the candles lighting her face, the room deathly
still. Then she arose, and with her eyes half
shut, and her lips moving as if with her unfin-
ished prayer, she lifted her head and kissed me
on the forehead, on the chin, and on each cheek,
making with her finger the sign of the cross.
Then, reaching for a pair of scissors, and cutting
a small tress from her hair, she closed the locket
upon it, and laid it in my hand.

" Early the next morning I was at her door.
She was dressed and waiting. She greeted me
kindly, but mournfully, saying in a tone which
denoted her belief in its impossibility : —

" ' And you will not go to Cracow ? '

" When we reached the station, and I halted
at the small gate opening upon the train platform, she merely pressed my hand, covered her
head with her veil, and entered the carriage,
followed by Polaff. I watched, hoping to see her
face at the window, but she remained hidden.

" I turned into the Ringstrasse, still filled

with her presence, and, tortured by the thought
of the conditions that prevented my following
her, called a cab, and drove to our minister's.
Mr. Motley then held the portfolio; my passport had expired, and, as I was entering Germany, needed renewing. The attaché agreed
to the necessity, stamped it, and brought it
back to me with the ink still wet.

" 'His excellency,' said he, ' advises extreme
caution on your part while here. Be careful of
your associates, and keep out of suspicious company. Vienna is full of spies watching escaped
Polish refugees. Your name ' — reading it carefully — ' is apt to excite remark. We are pow-
erless to help in these cases. Only last week
an American who befriended a man in the street
was arrested on the charge of giving aid and comfort to the enemy, and, despite our efforts, is
still in prison.'

"I thanked him, and regained my cab with
my head whirling. What, after all, if the countess should have deceived me ? My blood chilled
as I remembered her words of the day before :
recalled by the government she hated, her two
brothers forced into the army, the cruelties and
indignities Russia had heaped upon her family,
and this last peremptory order to return. Had
my sympathetic nature and inexperience gotten

me into trouble ? Then that Madonna-like head with angelic face, the lips moving in prayer, rose before me. No, no ; not she. I would stake my life.

"I entered my hotel, and walked across the corridor for the key of my room. Standing by the porter was an Austrian officer in full uniform, even to his white kid gloves. As I passed I heard the porter say in German : —

"'Yes ; that is the man.'

"The Austrian looked at me searchingly, and, wheeling around sharply, said : —

"'Monsieur, can I see you alone ? I have something of importance to communicate.'

"The remark and his abrupt manner indicated so plainly an arrest, that for the moment I hesitated, running over in my mind what might be my wisest course to pursue. Then, thinking I could best explain my business in Vienna in the privacy of my room, I said stiffly : —

"'Yes ; I am now on my way to my apartment. I will see you there.'

"He entered first, shut the door behind him, crossed the room ; passed his hand behind the curtains, opened the closet, shut it, and said : —

"'We are alone ? '

" ' Quite.'

" Then, confronting me, ' You are an American ? '

" ' You are right.'

" ' And have your passport with you ? '

" I drew it from my pocket, and handed it to
him. He glanced at the signature, refolded it,
and said : —

" ' You took the Countess Smolenski to the
station this morning. Where did you meet
her ? '

" ' On the train yesterday leaving Venice.'

" ' Never before ? '

" ' Never.'

" ' Why did she not leave Venice earlier ? '

" ' The count was dying, and could not be
moved. He was buried two days ago.'

" A shade passed over his face. ' Poor De
Rescka ! I suspected as much.'

" Then facing me again, his face losing its
suspicious expression : —

" ' Monsieur, I am the brother of the countess,
— Colonel Boski of the army. A week ago my
letters were intercepted, and I left Cracow in
the night. Since then I have been hunted like
an animal. This uniform is my third disguise.
As soon as my connection with the plot was
discovered, my sister was ordered home. The

death of the count explains her delay, and prevented my seeing her at the station. I had selected the first station out of Vienna. I tried for an opportunity this morning at the depot, but dared not. I saw you, and learned from the cabman your hotel.'

"'But, colonel,' said I, the attaché's warning in my ears, ' you will pardon me, but these are troublous times. I am alone here, on my way to Berlin to pursue my studies. I found the countess ill and suffering, and unable to sleep. She interested me profoundly, and I did what I could to relieve her. I would have done the same for any other woman in her condition the world over, no matter what the consequences. If you are her brother, you will appreciate this. If you are here for any other purpose, say so at once. I leave Vienna at noon.'

" His color flushed, and his hand instinctively felt for his sword ; then, relaxing, he said : —

"'You are right. The times are troublous. Every other man is a spy. I do not blame you for suspecting me. I have nothing but my word. If you do not believe it, I cannot help it. I will go. You will at least permit me to thank you for your kindness to my sister,' drawing off his glove and holding out his hand.

"' The hand of a soldier is never refused the

world over,' and I shook it warmly. As it dropped to his side I caught sight of his seal ring.

" 'Pardon me one moment. Give me your hand again.' The ring bore the crest and motto of the countess.

" 'It is enough, colonel. Your sister showed me her own on the train. Pardon my suspicions. What can I do for you ? '

"He looked puzzled, hardly grasping my meaning.

" 'Nothing. You have told me all I wanted to know.'

" 'But you will breakfast with me before I take the train ? ' I said.

" 'No; that might get you into trouble — serious trouble, if I should be arrested. On the contrary, I must insist that you remain in this room until I leave the building.'

" 'But you perhaps need money ; these disguises are expensive,' glancing at his perfect appointment.

" 'You are right. Perhaps twenty rubles — it will be enough. Give me your address in Berlin. If I am taken, you will lose your money. If I escape, it will be returned.'

"I shook his hand, and the door closed. A week later a man wrapped in a cloak called at my lodgings and handed me an envelope. There was no address and no message, only twenty rubles."

I looked out over the sea wrinkling below me like a great sheet of gray satin. The huge life-boat swung above our heads, standing out in strong relief against the sky. After a long pause, — the story had strangely thrilled me, — I asked : —

" Pardon me, have you ever seen or heard of the countess since ? "

" Never."

" Nor her brother ? "

" Nor her brother."

" And the locket ? "

" It is here where she placed it."

At this instant the moon rolled out from behind a cloud, and shone full on his face. He drew out his watch-chain, touched it with his thumb-nail, and placed the trinket in my hand. It was such as a child might wear, an enamelled thread encircling it. Through the glass I could see the tiny nest of jet-black hair.

For some moments neither of us spoke. At last, with my heart aglow, my whole nature profoundly stirred by the unconscious nobility of the man, I said : —

"My friend, do you know why she bound the bracelet to your wrist?"

"No; that always puzzled me. I have often wondered."

"She bound the bracelet to your wrist, as of old a maid would have wound her scarf about the shield of her victorious knight, as the queen would pin the iron cross to the breast of a hero. You were the first gentleman she had ever known in her life."

THE LADY OF LUCERNE

I

ABOVE the Schweizerhof Hotel, and at the end of the long walk fronting the lake at Lucerne, — the walk studded with the round, dumpy, Noah's-ark trees, — stands a great building surrounded by flowers and palms, and at night ablaze with hundreds of lamps hung in festoons of blue, yellow, and red. This is the Casino. On each side of the wide entrance is a bill-board, announcing that some world-renowned Tyrolean warbler, famous acrobat, or marvellous juggler will sing or tumble or bewilder, the price of admission remaining the same, despite the enormous sum paid for the appearance of the performer.

Inside this everybody's club is a café, with hurrying waiters and a solid brass band, and opening from its smoke and absinthe laden interior blazes a small theatre, with stage foot-lights and scenery, where the several world-renowned artists redeem at a very considerable discount the promissory notes of the bill-boards outside.

During the performance the audience smoke and sip. Between the acts most of them swarm out into the adjacent corridors leading to the gaming - rooms, — licensed rooms these, with toy horses ridden by tin jockeys, and another equally delusive and tempting device of the devil, — a game of tipsy marbles, rolling about in search of sunken saucers emblazoned with the arms of the nations of the earth. These whirligigs of amateur crime are constantly surrounded by eager-eyed men and women, who try their luck for the amusement of the moment, or by broken-down, seedy gamblers, hazarding their last coin for a turn of fortune. Now and then, too, some sweet-faced girl, her arm in her father's, wins a louis with a franc, her childish laughter ringing out in the stifling atmosphere.

The Tyrolean warbler had just finished her high-keyed falsetto, bowing backward in her short skirts and stout shoes with silver buckles, and I had just reached the long corridor on my way to the garden, to escape the blare and pound of the band, when a man leaned out of a half-opened door and touched my shoulder.

"Pardon, monsieur. May I speak to you a moment?"

He was a short, thick-set, smooth-shaven, greasy man, dressed plainly in black, with a huge emerald pin in his shirt-front. I have never had any particular use for a man with an emerald pin in his shirt-front.

"There will be a game of baccarat," he continued in a low voice, his eyes glancing about furtively, "at eleven o'clock precisely. Knock twice at this door."

Old habitués of Lucerne — habitués of years, men who never cross the Alps without at least a day's stroll under the Noah's-ark trees — will tell you over their coffee that since the opening of the St. Gotthard Tunnel this half-way house of Lucerne — this oasis between Paris and Rome — has sheltered most of the adventurers of Europe; that under these same trees, and on these very benches, nihilists have sat and plotted, refugees and outlaws have talked in whispers, and adventuresses, with jewelled stilettos tucked in their bosoms, have lain in wait for fresher victims.

I had never in my wanderings met any of these mysterious and delightful people. And, strange to say, I had never seen a game of baccarat. This might be my opportunity. I would see the game and perhaps run across some of these curious individuals. I consulted my watch; there was half an hour yet. The man was a runner, of course, for this underground, unlicensed gaming-house, who had picked me out as a possible victim.

When the moment arrived I knocked at the door.

It was opened, not by the greasy Jack-in-the-box with the emerald pin, but by a deferential old man, who looked at me for a moment, holding the door with his foot. Then gently closing it, he preceded me across a hall and up a long staircase. At the top was a passageway and another door, and behind this a large room panelled in dark wood. On one side of this apartment was a high desk. Here sat the cashier counting money, and arranging little piles of chips of various colors. In the centre stood a table covered with black cloth : I had always supposed such tables to be green. About it were seated ten people, the croupier in the middle. The game had already begun. I moved up a chair, saying that I would look on, but not play.

Had the occasion been a clinic, the game a corpse, and the croupier the operating surgeon, the group about the table could not have been more absorbed or more silent, — a cold, death-

like, ominous stillness that seemed to saturate
the very air. The only sounds were the oc-
casional clickings of the ivory chips, like the
chattering of teeth, and the monotones of the
croupier announcing the results of the play : —

"Faites vos jeux. Le jeu est fait ; rien ne
va plus."

I began to study the *personnel* of this clinic
of chance.

Two Englishmen in evening dress sat side by
side, never speaking, scarcely moving, their
eyes riveted on the falling cards flipped from
the croupier's hands. A coarse-featured, oily-
skinned woman — a Russian, I thought —
looked on calmly, resting her head on her palm.
A man in a gray suit, with waxy face and wa-
tery, yellow eyes, made paper pills, rolling them
slowly between thumb and forefinger — his
features as immobile as a death-mask. A blue-
eyed, blond-haired German, with a decoration
on the lapel of his coat, nonchalantly twirled
his mustache, his shoulders straining in tension.
A Parisienne, with bleached hair and pencilled
eyebrows, leaned over her companion's arm.
There was also a flashily dressed negro, evidently a Haytian, who sat motionless at the far
end, as stolid as a boiler, only the steam-gauge
of his eyes denoting the pressure beneath.

No one spoke, no one laughed.

Two of the group interested me at once, — the croupier and a woman who sat within three feet of me.

The croupier, who was in evening dress, might have been of any age from thirty to fifty. His eyes were deep-set and glassy, like those of a consumptive. His hair was jet-black, his face clean-shaven ; the skin, not ivory, but a dirty white, and flabby, like the belly of a toad. His thin and bloodless lips were flattened over a row of pure white teeth with glistening specks of gold that opened when he smiled ; closing again slowly like an automaton's. His shrunken, colorless hands lay on the black cloth like huge white spiders ; their long, thin legs of fingers turned up at the tips — stealthy, creeping fingers. Sometimes, too, in their nervous workings, they drooped together like a bunch of skeleton keys. On one of these lock picks he wore a ring studded alternately with diamonds and rubies.

The cards seemed to know these fingers, fluttering about them, or lighting noiselessly at their bidding on the cloth.

When the bank won, the croupier permitted a slight shade of disappointment to flash over his face, fading into an expression of apology for taking the stakes. When the bank lost, the lips parted slowly, showing the teeth, in a half smile. Such delicate outward consideration for the feelings of his victims seemed a part of his education, an index to his natural refinement.

The woman was of another type. Although she sat with her back to me, I could catch her profile when she pushed her long veil from her face. She was dressed entirely in black. She had been, and was still, a woman of marked beauty, with an air of high breeding which was unmistakable. Her features were clean-cut and refined, her mouth and nose delicately shaped. Her forehead was shaded by waves of brown hair which half covered her ears. The eyes were large and softened by long lashes, the lids red as if with recent weeping. Her only ornament was a plain gold ring, worn on her left hand. Outwardly, she was the only person in the room who betrayed by her manner any vital interest in the game.

There are some faces that once seen haunt you forever afterward, — faces with masks so thinly worn that you look through into the heart below. Hers was one of these. Every light and shadow of hope and disappointment that crossed it showed only the clearer the intensity of her mental strain, and the bitterness of her anxiety.

Once when she lost she bit her lips so deeply that a speck of blood tinged her handkerchief. The next instant she was clutching her winnings with almost the ferocity of a hungry animal. Then she leaned back a moment later exhausted in her chair, her face thrown up, her eyes closing wearily.

In her hand she held a small chamois bag filled with gold ; when her chips were exhausted she would rise silently, float like a shadow to the desk, lay a handful of gold from the bag upon the counter, sweep the ivories into her hand, and noiselessly regain her seat. She seemed to know no one, and no one to know her, unless it might have been the croupier, who, I thought, watched her closely when he pushed over her winnings, parting his lips a little wider, his smile a trifle more cringing and devilish.

At twelve o'clock she was still playing, her face like chalk, her eyes bloodshot, her teeth clenched fast, her hair dishevelled across her face.

The game went on.

When the clock reached the half-hour the man in gray pushed back his chair, gathered up his winnings, and moved to the door, an attendant handing him his hat. With the exception of the Parisienne, who had gone some time before, taking her companion with her, the devotees were the same, — the two Englishmen still exchanging clean, white Bank of England notes, the German and Haytian losing, but calm as mummies, the fat, oily woman melting like a red candle, the perspiration streaming down her face.

Suddenly I heard a convulsive gasp. The woman in black was on her feet, leaning over the table. Her eyes blazed in a frenzy of delight. She was sweeping into her open hands the piles of gold before her. By some marvellous stroke of luck, and with almost her last louis, she had won every franc on the cloth !

Then she drew herself up defiantly, covered her face with her veil, hugged the money to her breast, and staggered from the room.

II

So deep an impression had the gambling scene of the night before made upon me that the next morning I loitered under the Noah's-ark trees, hoping I might identify the woman, and in some impossible, improbable way know more of her history. I even lounged into the Casino, tried

the door at which I had knocked the night before, and, finding it locked and the scrubwoman
suspicious, strolled out carelessly into the garden, and, sitting down under the palms, tried
to pick out the windows that opened into the
gaming-room. But they were all alike, with
pots of flowers blooming in each.

Still burdened with these memories, I entered
the church, — the old church with square towers and deep-receding entrance, that stands on
the crest of a steep hill overlooking the Casino,
and within a short distance of the Noah's-ark
trees. Every afternoon, near the hour of twilight, when the shadows reach down Mount
Pilatus, and the mists gather in the valley, a
broken procession of strollers, in twos and threes
and larger groups, slowly climb its path. They
are on their way to hear the great organ played.
The audience was already seated. It was at
the moment of that profound hush which pre-
cedes the recital. Even my footfall, light as it
was, reëchoed to the groined arches. The church
was ghostly dark, — so dark that the hundreds
of heads melted into the mass of pews, and
they into the gloom of column and wall. The
only distinguishable gleam was the soft glow
of the dying day struggling through the lower
panes of the dust-begrimed windows. Against

these hung long chains holding unlighted lamps.

I felt my way to an empty pew on a side aisle, and sat down. The silence continued. Now and again there was a slight cough, instantly checked. Once a child dropped a book, the echoes lasting apparently for minutes. The darkness became almost black night. Only the clean, new panes of glass used in repairing some break in the begrimed windows showed clear. These seemed to hang out like small square lanterns.

Suddenly I was aware that the stillness was broken by a sound faint as a sigh, delicate as the first breath of a storm. Then came a great sweep growing louder, the sweep of deep thunder tones with the roar of the tempest, the rush of the mighty rain, the fury of the avalanche, the voices of the birds singing in the sunlight, the gurgle of the brooks, and the soft cadence of the angelus calling the peasants to prayers. Next a pause and another burst of melody, ending in profound silence, as if the door of heaven had been opened and as quickly shut. Now a clear voice springing into life, singing like a lark, rising, swelling — up — up — filling the church — the roof — the sky! Then the heavenly door thrown wide, and the melody pouring out in a torrent, drowning the voice. And then above it all, while I sat quivering, there soared like a bird in the air, singing as it flew, one great, superb, vibrating, resolute note, pure, clear, full, sensuous, untrammelled, dominating the heavens : not human, not divine ; like no woman's, like no man's, like no angel's ever dreamed of, — the vox humana.

It did not awaken in me any feeling of reverence or religious ecstasy. I only remember that the music took possession of my soul. That beneath and through it all I felt the vibrations of all the tragic things that come to men and women in their lives. Scenes from out an irrelevant past swept across my mind. I heard again the long winding note of the bugle echoing through the pines, the dead in uneven rows, the moon lighting their faces. I caught once more the cry of the girl my friend loved, he who died and never knew. I saw the quick plunge of the strong swimmer, white arms clinging to his neck, and heard once more that joyous shout from a hundred throats. And I could still hear the hoarse voice of the captain with drenched book and flickering lantern, and shivered again as I caught the dull splash of the sheeted body dropping into the sea.

The vox humana stopped, not gradually but

abruptly, as if the heart had broken and its life had gone out in the one supreme effort. Then silence, — a silence so profound that a low sob from the pew across the aisle startled me. I strained my eyes, and caught the outlines of a woman heavily veiled. I could see, too, a child beside her, his head on her shoulder. The boy was bare-headed, his curls splashed over her black dress. Then another sob, half smothered, as if the woman were strangling.

No other sound broke the stillness; only the feeling everywhere of pent-up, smothered sighs.

In this intense moment a faint footfall was heard approaching from the church door, walking in the gloom. It proved to be that of an old man, bent and trembling. He came slowly down the sombre church, with unsteady, shambling gait, holding in one hand a burning taper, — a mere speck. In the other he carried a rude lantern, its wavering light hovering about his feet. As he passed in his long brown cloak, the swaying light encircled his white beard and hair with a fluffy halo. He moved slowly, the spark he carried no larger than a firefly. The sacristan had come to light the candles.

He stopped halfway down the middle aisle, opposite a pew, the faint flush of his lantern falling on the nearest upturned face. A long, thin candle was fastened to this pew. The fire-fly of a taper, held aloft in his trembling hand, flickered uncertainly like a moth and rested on the top of this candle. Then the wick kindled and burned. As its rays felt their way over the vast interior, struggling up into the dark roof, reaching the gilded ornaments on the side altar enshrouded in gloom, glinting on the silver of the hanging lamps, a plaintive note fluttered softly, swelled into an ecstasy of sound, and was lost in a chorus of angel voices.

The sacristan moved down the aisle, kindled two other candles on the distant altar, and was lost in the shadows.

The woman in the pew across the aisle bent forward, resting her head on the back of the seat in front, drawing the child to her. The boy cuddled closer. As she turned, a spark of light trickled down her cheek. I caught sight of the falling tear, but could not see the face.

The music ceased ; the last anthem had been played ; a gas-jet flared in the organ-loft ; the people began to rise from their seats. The sac-ristan appeared again from behind the altar, and walked slowly down the side aisle, carrying only his lantern. As he neared my seat the woman stood erect, and passed out of the pew, her hand

caressing the child. Surely I could not be mistaken about that movement, the slow, undulat-
ing rhythmic walk, the floating shadow of the
night before. Certainly not with the light of
the sacristan's lantern now full on her face.
Yes: the same finely chiselled features, the
same waves of brown hair, the same eyes, the
same drooping eyelids, like blossoms wet with
dew ! At last I had found her.

I walked behind, — so close that I could have
laid my hand on her boy's head, or touched
her hand as it lay buried in his curls. The old,
bent sacristan stepped in front, swinging his
lantern, the ghostly shadows wavering about
his feet. Then he halted to let the crowd clear
the main aisle.

As he stood still, the woman drew suddenly
back as if stunned by a blow, clutched the
boy to her side, and fixed her eyes on the lantern's ghostly shadows. I leaned over quickly.
The glow of the rude lamp, with its squares
of waving light flecking the stone flagging,
traced in unmistakable outlines the form of a
cross !

For some minutes she stood as if in a trance,
her eyes fastened upon the floating shadow, her
whole form trembling, bent, her body swaying.
Only when the sacristan moved a few paces

ahead to hold open the swinging door, and the shadow of the cross faded, did she awake from the spell.

Then, recovering herself slowly, she bowed reverently, crossed herself, drew the boy closer, and, with his hand in hers, passed out into the cool starlit night.

III

The following morning I was sitting under the Noah's-ark trees, watching the people pass and repass, when a man in a suit of white flannel, carrying a light cane, and wearing a straw hat with a red band, and a necktie to match, stopped a flower-girl immediately in front of me, and affixed an additional dot of blood-color to his buttonhole.

In the glare of the daylight he was even more yellow than when under the blaze of the gas-jets. His eyes were still glassy and brilliant, but the rims showed red, as if for want of sleep, and beneath the lower lids lay sunken half-circles of black. He moved with his wonted precision, but without that extreme gravity of manner which had characterized him the night of the game. Looked at as a mere passer-by, he would have impressed you as a rather debonair, overdressed habitué, who was enjoying his

morning stroll under the trees, without other
purpose in life than the breathing of the cool
air and enjoyment of the attendant exercise.
His spidership had doubtless seen me when he
entered the walk, — I was still an untrapped
fly, — and had picked out this particular flower-
girl beside me as a safe anchorage for one end
of his web. I turned away my head ; but it
was too late.

"Monsieur did not play last night ? " the
croupier asked deferentially.

"No ; I did not know the game." Then an
idea struck me. "Sit down ; I want to talk to
you." He touched the edge of his hat with one
finger, opened a gold cigarette-case studded with
jewels, offered me its contents, and took the
seat beside me.

"Pardon the abruptness of the inquiry, but
who was the woman in black ? " I asked.

He looked at me curiously.

"Ah, you mean madame with the bag ? "

"Yes."

"She was once the Baroness Frontignac."

"Was once ! What is she now ? "

"Now ? Ah, that is quite a story."

He stopped, shut the gold case with a click,
and leaned forward, flicking the pebbles with
the point of his cane. " If madame had had a

147

larger bag she might have broken the bank. Is it not so ? "

" You know her, then ? " I persisted.

" Monsieur, men of my profession know everybody. Sooner or later they all come to us — when they are young, and their francs have wings ; when they are gray-haired and cautious ; when they are old and foolish."

" But she did not look like a gambler," I replied stiffly.

He smiled his old cynical, treacherous smile.

" Monsieur is pleased to be very pronounced in his language. A gambler ! Monsieur no doubt means to say that madame has not the appearance of being under the intoxication of the play." Then with a positive tone, still flicking the pebbles, " The baroness played for love."

" Of the cards ? " I asked persistently. I was determined to drive the nail to the head.

The croupier looked at me fixedly, shrugged his shoulders, laughed between his teeth, a little, hissing laugh that sounded like escaping steam, and said slowly : —

" No; of a man."

Then, noticing my increasing interest, " Monsieur would know something of madame ? "

He held up his hand, and began crooking one finger after another as he recounted her history.

These bent keys, it seemed, unlocked secrets as well.

"Le voilà! the drama of Madame la Baronne! The play opens when she is first a novice in the convent of Saint Ursula, devoted to good works and the church. Next you find her a grand dame and rich, the wife of Baron Alphonse de Frontignac, first secretary of legation at Vienna. Then a mother with one child, — a boy, now six or seven years old, who is hardly ever out of her arms." He stopped, toyed for a moment with his match-safe, slipped it into his pocket, and said carelessly, "So much for Act I."

Then, after a pause during which he traced again little diagrams in the gravel, he said suddenly : —

"Does this really interest you, monsieur ? "

"Unquestionably."

"You know her, then ? " This with a glance of suspicion as keen as it was unexpected by me.

"Never saw her in my life before," I answered frankly, "and never shall again. I leave for Paris to-day, and sail from Havre on Saturday."

He drew in the point of his cane, looked me all over with one of those comprehensive sweeps

149

of the eye, as if he would read my inmost thought, and then, with an expression of confidence born doubtless of my evident sincerity, continued : —

"In the next act Frontignac gets mixed up in some banking scandals, — he would, like a fool, play roulette; baccarat was always his strong game, — disappears from Vienna, is arrested at the frontier, escapes, and is found the next morning under a brush-heap with a bullet through his head. This ends the search. Two years later — this is now Act III. — Madame la Baronne, without a sou to her name, is hard at work in the hospitals of Metz. The child is pensioned out near by.

"Now comes the grand romance. An officer attached to the 13th Cuirassiers — a regiment with not men enough left after Metz to muster a company — is picked up for dead, with one arm torn off, and a sabre-slash over his head, and brought to her ward. She nurses him back to life, inch by inch, and in six months he joins his regiment. Now please follow the plot. It is quite interesting. Is it not easy to see what will happen ? Tender and beautiful, young and brave ! Vive le bel amour ! It is the old story, but it is also une affaire de cœur — la grande passion. In a few months they are married, and

he takes her to his home in Rouen. There he
listens to her entreaties, and resigns his com-
mission.

"This was five years ago. To-day he is a
broken-down man, starving on his pension ; a
poor devil about the streets, instead of a general
commanding a department ; and all for love of
her. Some, of course, said it was the sabre-cut ;
some that he could no longer hold his command,
he was so badly slashed. But it is as I tell you.
You can see him here any day, sitting under the
trees, playing with the child, or along the lake
front, leaning on her arm."

Here the croupier rose from the bench, looked
critically over his case of cigarettes, selected
one carefully, and began buttoning his coat as
if to go.

By this time I had determined to know the
end. I felt that he had told me the truth as far
as he had gone ; but I felt, also, that he had
stopped at the most critical point of her career.
I saw, too, that he was familiar with its details.

"Go on, please. Here, try a cigar." My interest in my heroine had even made me courteous. My aversion to him, too, was wearing off.
Perhaps, after all, croupiers were no worse than
other people. "Now one thing more. Why
was she in your gambling-house ? "

He lighted the cigar, touched his hat with his forefinger, and again seated himself.

" Well, then, monsieur, as you will. I always trust you Americans. When you lose, you pay ; when you win, you keep your mouths shut. Besides,'' — this was spoken more to himself, — "you have never seen him, and never will. Le voilà. One night, — this only a year ago, remember, — in one of the gardens at Baden, a hand touched the baroness's shoulder.

" It was *Frontignac's.*

" The body under the brush-heap had been that of another man dressed in Frontignac's clothes. The bullet-hole in his head was made by a ball from Frontignac's pistol. Since then he had been hiding in exile.

" He threatened exposure. She pleaded for her boy and her crippled husband. She could, of course, have handed him over to the nearest gendarme ; but that meant arrest, and arrest meant exposure. At their home in Vienna, let me tell you, baccarat had been played nightly as a pastime for their guests. So great was her luck that ' as lucky as the Baronne Frontignac ' was a byword. Frontignac's price was this : she must take his fifty louis and play that stake at the Casino that night ; when she brought him ten thousand francs he would vanish.

"That night at Baden — I was dealing, and know — she won twelve thousand francs in as many minutes. Here her slavery began. It will continue until Frontignac is discovered and captured; then he will put a second bullet into his own head. When I saw her enter my room I knew he had turned up again. As she staggered out, one of my men shadowed her. I was right; Frontignac was skulking in the garden."

All my disgust for the croupier returned in an instant. He was still the same bloodless spider of the night before. I could hardly keep my hands off him.

"And you permit this, and let this woman suffer these tortures, her life made miserable by this scoundrel, when a word, even a look, from you would send him out of the country and " —

"Softly, monsieur, softly. Why blame me? What business is it of mine? Do I love the cripple? Have I robbed the bank and murdered my double? This is not my game; it is Frontignac's. Would you have me kick over his chessboard?"

BROCKWAY'S HULK

I FIRST saw Brockway's towards the close of a cold October day. Since early morning I had been tramping and sketching about the northern suburbs of New York, and it was late in the afternoon when I reached the edge of that high ground overlooking the two rivers. I could see through an opening in the woods the outline of the great aqueduct, — a huge stone centipede stepping across on its sturdy legs ; the broad Hudson, with its sheer walls of rock, and the busy Harlem crowded with boats and braced with bridges. A raw wind was blowing, and a gray mist blurred the edges of the Palisades where they cut against the sky.

As the darkness fell the wind increased ; and scattered drops of rain, piloting the coming storm, warned me to seek a shelter. Shouldering my trap and hurrying forward, I descended the hill, followed the road to the East River, and, finding no boat, walked along the shore, hoping to hail a fisherman or some belated oarsman, and reach the station opposite.

My search led me around a secluded cove edged with white sand and yellow marsh grass, ending in a low, jutting point. Here I came upon a curious sort of dwelling, — half house, half boat. It might have passed for an abandoned barge or wharf boat, too rotten to float and too worthless to break up, — the relic and record of some by-gone tide of phenomenal height. When I approached nearer it proved to be an old-fashioned canal-boat, sunk to the water line in the grass, its deck covered by a low-hipped roof. Midway its length was cut a small door, opening upon a short staging or portico which supported one end of a narrow, rambling bridge leading to the shore. This bridge was built of driftwood propped up on shad poles. Over the door itself flapped a scrap of a tattered sail which served as an awning. Some pots of belated flowers bloomed on the sills of the ill-shaped windows, and a wind-beaten vine, rooted in a fish basket, crowded into the door, as if to escape the coming winter. Nothing could have been more dilapidated or more picturesque.

The only outward sign of life about the dwelling was a curl of blue smoke. Without this signal of good cheer it had a menacing look, as it lay in its bed of mud glaring at me from under its eaves of eyebrows, shading eyes of windows a-glint in the fading light.

I crossed the small beach strewn with oyster shells, ascended the tottering bridge, and knocked. The door was opened by a gray-bearded old man in a rough jacket. He was barefooted, his trousers rolled up above his ankles, like a boy's.

"Can you help me across the river?" I asked.

"Yes, perhaps I can. Come into the Hulk," he replied, holding the door against the gusts of wind.

The room was small and low, with doors leading into two others. In its centre, before a square stove, stood a young child cooking the evening meal. I saw no other inmates.

"You are wet," said the old man, laying his hand on my shoulder, feeling me over carefully; "come nearer the stove."

The child brought a chair. As I dropped into it I caught his eye fixed upon me intently.

"What are you?" he said abruptly, noting my glance, — "a pedler?" He said this standing over me, — his arms akimbo, his bare feet spread apart.

"No, a painter," I answered, smiling; my trap had evidently misled him.

156

He mused a little, rubbing his beard with his thumb and forefinger; then, making a mental inventory of my exterior, beginning with my slouch hat and taking in each article down to my tramping shoes, he said slowly: —

" And poor ? "

" Yes, we all are." And I laughed; his manner made me a little uncomfortable.

My reply, however, seemed to reassure him. His features relaxed and a more kindly expression overspread his countenance.

" And now, what are *you* ? " I asked, offering him a cigarette as I spoke.

" Me ? Nothing," he replied curtly, refusing it with a wave of his hand. " Only Brockway, — just Brockway, — that's all, just Brockway." He kept repeating this in an abstracted way, as if the remark was addressed to himself, the words dying in his throat.

Then he moved to the door, took down an oilskin from a peg, and saying that he would get the boat ready, went out into the night, shutting the door behind him, his bare feet flapping like wet fish as he walked.

I was not sorry I was going away so soon. The man and the place seemed uncanny.

I roused myself and crossed the room, attracted by the contents of a cupboard filled with

157

cheap pottery and some bits of fine old English lustre. Then I examined the furniture of the curious interior, — the high-backed chairs, mahogany table, — one leg replaced with pine, — the hair sofa and tall clock in the corner by the door. They were all old and once costly, and all of a pattern of by-gone days. Everything was scrupulously clean, even to the strip of unbleached muslin hung at the small windows.

The door blew in with a whirl of wind, and Brockway entered, shaking the wet from his sou'wester.

"You must wait," he said. "Dan the brakeman has taken my boat to the Railroad Dock. He will return in an hour. If you are hungry, you can sup with us. Emily, set a place for the painter."

His manner was more frank. He seemed less uncanny, too. Perhaps he had been in some special ill humor when I entered. Perhaps, too, he had been suspicious of me; I had not thought of that before.

The child spread the cloth and busied herself with the dishes and plates. She was about twelve years old, slightly built and neatly dressed. Her eyes were singularly large and expressive. The light brown hair about her

158

shoulders held a tinge of gold when the lamp-light shone upon it.

Despite the evident poverty of the interior, a certain air of refinement pervaded everything. Even the old man's bare feet did not detract from it. These, by the way, he never referred to ; it was evidently a habit with him. I felt this refinement not only in the relics of what seemed to denote better days, but in the arrangement of the table, the placing of the tea tray, and the providing of a separate pot for the hot water. Their voices, too, were low, characteristic of people who live alone and in peace, — especially the old man's.

Brockway resumed his seat and continued talking, asking about the city as if it were a thousand miles away instead of being almost at his door ; of the artists, their mode of life, their successes, etc. As he talked his eye brightened and his manner became more gentle. It was only his outside that seemed to belong to an old boatman, roughened by the open air, with hands hard and brown. Yet these were well shaped, with tapering fingers. One bore a gold ring curiously marked and worn to a thread.

I asked about the fishing, hoping the subject would lead him to talk of his own life, and so solve the doubt in my mind as to his class and antecedents. His replies showed his thorough knowledge of his trade. He deplored the scarcity of bass, now that the steamboats and factories fouled the river; the decrease of the oysters, of which he had several beds, — all being injured by the same cause. Then he broke out against the encroachments of the real estate pirates, as he called them, staking out lots behind the Hulk and destroying his privacy.

"But you own the marsh?" I asked carelessly. I saw instantly in his face the change working in his mind. He looked at me searchingly, almost fiercely, and said, weighing each word : —

"Not one foot, young man, — do you hear? — not one foot! Own nothing but what you see. But this hulk is mine, — mine from the mud to the ridgepole, with every rotten timber in it."

The outburst was so sudden that I rose from my chair. For a moment he seemed consumed with an inward rage, — not directed to me in any way, — more as if the memory of some past wrong had angered him.

Here the child, with an anxious face, rose quickly from her seat by the window, and laid her hand on his.

The old man looked into her face for a moment, and then, as if her touch had softened him, rose courteously, took her arm, seated her at the table and then me. In a moment more he had regained his gentle manner.

The meal was a frugal one, broiled fish and potatoes, a loaf of bread, and stewed apples served in a cut-glass dish with broken handles.

The meal over, the girl replaced the cotton cloth with a red one, retrimmed the lamps, and disappeared into an adjoining room, carrying the dishes. The old man lighted his pipe and seated himself in a large chair, smoking on in silence. I opened my portfolio and began retouching the sketches of the morning.

Outside the weather grew more boisterous. The wind increased; the rain thrashed against the small windows, the leakage dropping on the floor like the slow ticking of a clock.

As the evening wore on I began to be uneasy, speculating as to the possibility of my reaching home that night. To be entirely frank, I did not altogether like my surroundings or my host. One moment he was like a child; the next there came into his face an expression of uncontrollable hate that sent a shiver through me. But for the clear, steady gaze of his eye I should have doubted his sanity.

There was no sign of the return of the boat.
The old man became restless himself. He said
nothing, but every now and then he would peer
through the window and raise his hand to his
ear as if listening. It was evident that he did
not want me overnight if he could help it.
This partly reassured me.

Finally, he laid down his pipe, put on his oilskin again, lighted a lantern, and pulled the
door behind him, the wind struggling to force
an entrance.

In a few minutes he returned with lantern out,
the rain glistening on his white, bushy beard.
Without a word, he hung up his dripping garments, placed the lantern on the floor, and
called the child into the adjoining room. When
he came back, he laid his hand on my shoulder
and said, with a tone in his voice that was unmistakable in its sincerity : —

"I am sorry, friend, but the boat cannot get
back to-night. You seem like a decent man,
and I believe you are. I knew some of your kind ·
once, and I always liked them. You must stay
where you are to-night, and have Emily's room."

I thanked him, but hoped the weather would
clear. As to taking Emily's room, this I could
not do. I would not, of course, disturb the
child. If there was no chance of my getting

162

away, I said, I preferred taking the floor, with my trap for a pillow. But he would not hear of it. He was not accustomed, he said, to have people stay with him, especially of late years ; but when they did, they could not sleep on the floor.

The child's room proved to be the old cabin of the canal-boat, with the three steps leading down from the decks. The little slanting windows were still there, and so were the bunks, — or, rather, the lower one. The upper one had been altered into a sort of closet. On one side hung a row of shelves on which were such small knickknacks as a child always loves, — a Christmas card or two, some books, a pincushion backed with shells, a doll's bonnet, besides some trinkets and strings of beads. Next to this ran a row of hooks covered by a curtain of cheap calico, half concealing her few simple dresses, with her muddy little shoes and frayed straw hat in the farther corner.

Above the headboard hung the likeness of a woman with large eyes, her hair pushed back from a wide, high forehead. It was framed in an old-fashioned black frame with a gold mat. Not a beautiful face, but so interesting and so expressive that I looked at it half a dozen times before I could return it to its place.

Everything was as clean and fresh as care could make it. When I dropped to sleep, the tide was swashing the floor beneath me, the rain still sousing and drenching the little windows and the roof.

The following week, one crisp, fresh morning, I was again at the Hulk. My experience the night of the storm had given me more confidence in Brockway, although the mystery of his life was still impenetrable. As I rounded the point, the old man and little Emily were just pushing off in the boat. He was on his way to his oyster beds a short distance off, his grappling-tongs and basket beside him. In his quick, almost gruff way, he welcomed me heartily and insisted on my staying to dinner. He would be back in an hour with a mess of oysters to help out. "Somebody has been raking my beds and I must look after them," he called to me as he rowed away.

I drew my own boat well up on the gravel, out of reach of the making tide, and put my easel close to the water's edge. I wanted to paint the Hulk and the river with the bluffs beyond. Before I had blocked in my sky, I caught sight of Brockway rowing hurriedly back, followed by a shell holding half a dozen oarsmen

164

from one of the boating clubs down the river.
The crew were out for a spin in their striped
shirts and caps ; the coxswain was calling to
him, but he made no reply.

"Say, Mr. Brockway ! will you please fill
our water-keg? We have come off from the boat-
house without a drop," I heard one call out.

"No ; not to save your lives, I would n't ! "
he shouted back, his boat striking the beach.
Springing out and catching Emily by the shoul-
der, pushing her before him, "Go into the
Hulk, child." Then, lowering his voice to me,
"They are all alike, d——them, all alike.
Just such a gang! I know 'em, I know 'em.
Get you a drink ? I 'll see you dead first, d——
you. See you dead first ; do you hear ? "

His face was livid, his eyes blazing with anger. The crew turned and shot up the river,
grumbling as they went. Brockway unloaded
his boat, clutching the tongs as if they were
weapons ; then, tying the painter to a stake,
sat down and watched me at work. Soon Emily
crept back and slipped one hand around her
grandfather's neck.

"Do you think you can ever do that, little
Frowsy-head ? " he said, pointing to my sketch.
I looked up. His face was as serene and sunny
as that of the child beside him.

165

Gradually I came to know these people better. I never could tell why, our tastes being so
dissimilar. I fancied, sometimes, from a remark
the old man once made, that he had perhaps
known some one who had been a painter, and
that I reminded him of his friend, and on that
account he trusted me ; for I often detected him
examining my brushes, spreading the bristles
on his palm, or holding them to the light with
a critical air. I could see, too, that their touch
was not new to him.

As for me, the picturesqueness of the Hulk,
the simple mode of life of the inmates, their in-
nate refinement, the unselfish devotion of little
Emily to the old man, the conflicting elements
in his character, his fierceness — almost brutal-
ity — at times, his extreme gentleness at others,
his rough treatment of every stranger who at-
tempted to land on his shore, his tenderness
over the child, all combined to pique my curiosity to know something of his earlier life.

Moreover, I constantly saw new beauties in
the old Hulk. It always seemed to adapt itself
to the changing moods of the weather, — being
grave or gay as the skies lowered or smiled. In
the dull November days, when the clouds drifted
in straight lines of slaty gray, it assumed a
weird, forbidding look. When the wind blew

a gale from the northeast, and the back water of the river overflowed the marsh, —submerging the withered grass and breaking high upon the foot-bridge, — it seemed for all the world like the original tenement of old Noah himself, derelict ever since his disembarkation, and stranded here after centuries of buffetings. On other days it had a sullen air, settling back in its bed of mud as if tired out with all these miseries, glaring at you with its one eye of a window aflame with the setting sun.

As the autumn lost itself in the winter, I continued my excursions to the Hulk, sketching in the neighborhood, gathering nuts with little Emily, or helping the old man with his nets.

On one of these days a woman, plainly but neatly dressed, met me at the edge of the wood, inquired if I had seen a child pass my way, and quickly disappeared in the bushes. I noticed her anxious face and the pathos of her eyes when I answered. Then the incident passed out of my mind. A few days later I saw her again, sitting on a pile of stones as if waiting for some one. Little Emily had seen her too, and stopped to talk to her. I could follow their movements over my easel. As soon as the child caught my eye she started up and ran towards the Hulk, the woman darting again into the bushes. When

I questioned Emily about it she hesitated, and said it was a poor woman who had lost her little girl and who was very sad.

Brockway himself became more and more a mystery. I sought every opportunity to coax from him something of his earlier life, but he never referred to it but once, and then in a way that left the subject more impenetrable than ever.

I was speaking of a recent trip abroad when he turned abruptly and said : —

"Is the Milo still in that little room in the Louvre ?"

"Yes," I answered, surprised.

"I am glad of that. Against that red curtain she is the most beautiful thing I know."

"When did you see the Venus ?" I asked, as quietly as my astonishment would allow.

"Oh, some years ago, when I was abroad."

He was bending over and putting some new teeth in his oyster tongs at the time, riveting them on a flat-iron with a small hammer.

I agreed with him and asked carelessly what year that was and what he was doing in Paris, but he affected not to hear me and went on with his hammering, remarking that the oysters were running so small that some slipped through his tongs and he was getting too old to rake for them twice. It was only a glimpse of some part of his past, but it was all I could get. He never referred to it again.

December of that year was unusually severe. The snow fell early and the river was closed before Christmas. This shut off all communication with the Brockways except by the roundabout way I had first followed, over the hills from the west. So my weekly tramps ceased.

Late in the following February I heard, through Dan the brakeman, that the old man was greatly broken and had not been out of the Hulk for weeks. I started at once to see him. The ice was adrift and running with the tide, and the passage across was made doubly difficult by the floating cakes shelved one upon the other. When I reached the Hulk, the only sign of life was the thin curl of smoke from the rusty pipe. Even the snow of the night before lay unbroken on the bridge, showing that no foot had crossed it that morning. I knocked, and Emily opened the door.

"Oh, it's the painter, grandpa! We thought it might be the doctor."

He was sitting in an armchair by the fire, wrapped in a blanket. Holding out his hand, he motioned to a chair and said feebly : —

"How did you hear ?"

"The brakeman told me."

"Yes, Dan knows. He comes over Sundays."

He was greatly changed, — his skin drawn and shrunken, — his grizzled beard, once so great a contrast to his ruddy skin, only added to the pallor of his face. He had had a slight "stroke," he thought. It had passed off, but left him very weak.

I sat down and, to change the current of his thoughts, told him of the river outside, and the shelving ice, of my life since I had seen him, and whatever I thought would interest him. He made no reply, except in monosyllables, his head buried in his hands. Soon the afternoon light faded, and I rose to go. Then he roused himself, threw the blanket from his shoulders, and said in something of his old voice : —

"Don't leave me. Do you hear? Don't leave me!" this was with an authoritative gesture. Then, his voice faltering and with almost a tender tone, "Please help me through this. My strength is almost gone."

Later, when the night closed in, he called Emily to him, pushed her hair back and, kissing her forehead, said : —

"Now go to bed, little Frowsy-head. The painter will stay with me."

I filled his pipe, threw some dry driftwood in

the stove, and drew my chair nearer. He tried
to smoke for a moment, but laid his pipe down.
For some minutes he kept his eyes on the
crackling wood ; then, reaching his hand out,
laid it on my arm and said slowly : —

"If it were not for the child, I would be glad
that the end was near."

"Has she no one to care for her ? " I asked.

"Only her mother. When I am gone, she
will come."

"Her mother ? Why, Brockway ! I did not
know Emily's mother was alive. Why not send
for her now ? " I said, looking into his shrunken
face. "You need a woman's care at once."

His grasp tightened on my arm as he half
rose from the chair, his eyes blazing as I had
seen them that morning when he cursed the
boat's crew.

"But not that woman! Never, while I live!"
and he bent down his eyes on mine. "Look at
me. Men sometimes cut you to the quick, and
now and then a woman can leave a scar that
never heals ; but your own child, — do you
hear ; your little girl, the only one you ever
had, the one you laid store by and loved and
dreamed dreams of, — *she can tear your heart
out*. That 's what Emily's mother did for me.
Oh, a fine gentleman, with his yachts, and

171

boats, and horses, — a fine young aristocrat!
He was a thief, I tell you, a blackguard, a
beast, to steal my girl. Damn him! Damn him!
Damn him!" and he fell back in his chair exhausted.

"Where is she now?" I asked cautiously,
trying to change his thoughts. I was afraid of
the result if the outburst continued.

"God knows! Somewhere in the city. She
comes here every now and then," in a weaker
voice. "Emily meets her and they go off together when I am out raking my beds. Not long
ago I met her outside on the foot-bridge; she
did not look up; her hair is gray now, and her
face is thin and old, and so sad, — not as it
once was. God forgive me, — not as it once
was!" He leaned forward, his face buried in
his hands.

Then he staggered to his feet, took the lamp
from the table, and brought me the picture I
had seen in Emily's room the night of the
storm.

"You can see what she was like. It was
taken the year before his death, and came with
Emily's clothes. She found it in her box."

I held it to the light. The large, dreamy
eyes seemed even more pleading than when I
first had seen the picture; and the smooth hair

172

pushed back from the high forehead, I now saw, marked all the more clearly the lines of anxious care which were then beginning to creep over the sweet young face. It seemed to speak to me in an earnest, pleading way, as if for help.

"She is your daughter, Brockway, don't forget that."

He made no reply. After a pause, I went on, "And a girl's heart is not her own. Was it all her fault ? "

He pushed his chair back and stood erect, one hand raised above the other, clutching the blanket around his throat, the end trailing on the floor. By the flickering light of the dying fire he looked like some gaunt spectre towering above me, the blackness of the shadows only intensifying the whiteness of his face.

"Go on, go on. I know what you would say. You would have me wipe out the past and forget. Forget the home she ruined and the dead mother's heart she broke. Forget the weary months abroad, the tramping of London's streets looking into every woman's face, afraid it was she. Forget these years of exile and poverty, living here in this Hulk like a dog, my very name unknown. When I am dead they will say I have been cruel to her. God knows, perhaps I have ; listen ! " Then, glancing cautiously towards Emily's room and lowering his voice, he stooped down, his white sunken face close to mine, his eyes burning, gazed long and steadily into my face as if reading my very thoughts, and then, gathering himself up, said slowly: "No, no, I will not. Let it all be buried with me. I cannot, — cannot!" and sank into his chair.

After a while he raised his head, picked up the portrait from the table and looked into its eyes eagerly, holding it in both hands; and muttering to himself, crossed the room, and threw himself on his bed. I stirred the fire, wrapped my coat about me, and fell asleep on the lounge.

Later I awoke and crept to his bedside. He was lying on his back, the picture still clasped in his hands.

A week later, I reached the landing opposite the Hulk. There I met Dan's wife. Dan himself had been away for several days. She told me that two nights before she had been roused by a woman who had come up on the night express and wanted to be rowed over to the Hulk at once. She was in great distress, and did not mind the danger. Dan was against taking her, the ice being heavy and the night dark; but

174

she begged so hard he had not the heart to refuse her. She seemed to be expected, for Emily
was waiting with a lantern on the bridge and
put her arms around her and led her into the
Hulk.

Dan being away, I found another boatman,
and we pushed out into the river. I stood up
in the boat and looked over the waste of ice and
snow. Under the leaden sky lay the lifeless
Hulk. About the entrance and on the bridge
were black dots of figures, standing out in clear
relief like crows on the unbroken snow.

As I drew nearer, the dots increased in size
and fell into line, the procession slowly creeping along the tottering bridge, crunching the
snow under foot. Then I made out little Emily
and a neatly dressed woman heavily veiled.

When the shore was reached, I joined some
fishermen who stood about on the beach, uncovering their heads as the coffin passed. An
open wagon waited near the propped-up foot-
bridge of the Hulk, the horse covered with a
black blanket. Two men, carrying the body,
crouched down and pushed the box into the
wagon. The blanket was then taken from the
horse and wrapped over the pine casket.

The woman drew nearer and tenderly
smoothed its folds. Then she turned, lifted her

veil, and in a low voice thanked the few by-standers for their kindness.

It was the same face I had seen with Emily in the woods, — the same that lay upon his heart the last night I saw him alive.

WELL-WORN ROADS OF
SPAIN AND HOLLAND

INTRODUCTION

THESE sketches are the record of some idle days spent in rambling about odd places, and into quaint nooks, and along well-worn roads of travel. They contain no information of any value to anybody. They are absolutely bare of statistics, are entirely useless as a guide to travellers, and can be of no possible benefit to a student desirous of increasing his knowledge either of foreign architecture, mediæval art, politics, or any kindred subject.

They are not arranged in any order, have no specific bearing one upon the other, and are, in short, the merest outline of what one may see and hear who keeps both his eyes and his ears wide open.

They were written some months after the discomforts and annoyances of travel had passed out of mind, and when only the memory remained of the many happy hours spent under cool archways, and along canals, and up curious, twisted streets, and into dark, old, smoked churches. They, however, possess one quality, and that is truth.

A painter has peculiar advantages over other, less fortunate people. His sketch-book is a passport and his white umbrella a flag of truce in all lands under the sun, be it savage or civilized, — an " open sesame," bringing good cheer and hospitality, and entitling the possessor to all the benefits of liberty, equality, and fraternity.

I have been picked up on a roadside in Cuba by a Spanish grandee, who has driven me home in his volante to breakfast. I have been left in charge of the priceless relics and treasures of old Spanish churches hours at a time and alone. I have had my beer mug filled to the brim by mountaineers in the Tyrolean Alps, and had a chair placed for me at the table of a Dutchman living near the Zuider Zee. All these courtesies and civilities being the result of only ten minutes' previous acquaintance, and simply because I was a painter.

Truly " one touch of nature [with the brush] makes the whole world kin."

If, therefore, by reason of my craft and its advantages, I can show you some things you may perhaps have overlooked in your own wanderings, I shall be more than satisfied. So if

you will draw another easy-chair up to my
studio fire I will tell you as simply as I can
something of the groups who looked over my
shoulder while I worked, and who daily formed
my circle of acquaintance ; merely hinting to you
as delicately as possible that a traveller, even with
an ordinary pair of eyes and ears, can get much
nearer to the heart of a people in their cafés,
streets, and markets than in their museums,
galleries, and palaces, and reminding you at the
same time of the old adage which claims that
" a live gamin is better than a dead king," for
all the practical purposes of life.

F. H. S.

New York, September, 1886.

THE CHURCH OF SAN PABLO, SEVILLE

I HAD a queer adventure in this old Spanish church. I was a voluntary prisoner within its quiet walls for half a day. The intense heat of the morning had driven me out of the small plaza near the fruit market, and into a narrow, crooked street which led to the open church door. The interior was filled with the fragrant incense of the mass, just closed; and the cool air and silence of the place were so grateful that I laid my " trap " softly down near a group of pillars, uncovered my head, and watched the kneeling figures praying at the feet of the Virgin. Two altar boys entered from a side door, snuffed out the long candles, and covered the altar with white cloths. One by one the kneeling penitents rose, bowed reverently, drew their mantillas closer, and glided out into the sunlight.

Soon the sacristan appeared, closed the great swinging-doors behind the last worshipper, and discovered me with my easel up. I had already blocked in one end of the confessional, over which hung poised in air a huge angel, holding a swinging-lamp.

"Señor, it is not permitted to remain longer. It is eleven o'clock. At four you can return again."

Two pesetas performed a miracle. The sacristan was soon in the hot street with the money and the keys in his pocket, and I was locked up alone in the cool church with my easel and sketch. I continued painting. The hours wore on slowly. The light streamed in through the high windows, patterned the floor, crept up the altar steps, and illumined the head of the huge angel with a crown of prismatic color.

The silence became intense, and was broken only by the muffled sound of a door closing in the cloister beyond. Suddenly a panel opened in the solid wall to my left, and a figure closely veiled and shrouded in black tottered in, supported by her duenna and an elderly woman. She staggered to the altar steps, and threw back her mantilla. She was richly dressed, deathly pale, and her eyes red with weeping. With a cry of agony she lifted up her hands, and fell half swooning at the feet of the figure of the Virgin.

"Mi Adorada Amiga !" she sobbed, "they

have taken him away. Mother of God, have mercy!" The duenna raised her head and laid it in her lap. The mother sat silently by, smoothing her temples and fanning softly. Again she raised herself, and, winding her white arms around the Virgin, while her black hair streamed over her tear-stained face, she poured out her grief, until she sank back exhausted and motionless. This continued nearly an hour, — the señorita sobbing convulsively, and the two women kneeling beside her, waiting for the paroxysms to pass, until, utterly worn out, she was lifted and half carried across the aisle and through the open door. It closed gently and left no trace.

I emerged from my shelter, gathered up my brushes, and continued work. The confessional box took definite shape, and the angel was kept in his proper place by many pats of color bestowed on the background around him. A few touches brought out the swinging-lamp and the organ-pipes against the light high up in the nave. But I could not paint. I pushed back my easel and began wandering about. I sat down by the altar steps, near where the señorita had thrown herself, and examined carefully the poor cracked image of the Virgin, with the paint scaling off and crumbling under my touch, to which she had clung so desperately. I went on tiptoe to the altar. The old Spanish chairs on either side were covered with soiled linen covers; underneath, huge brass nails of a Moorish pattern, and scarlet velvet, threadbare. The vessels, quaint in design, silvered on copper. The cloths, superb with delicate Salamanca embroidery in pale yellow and white. The lamp which hung in front, suspended from a chain lost in the gloom of the roof, burned a ruby light. Behind the altar, broken saints of wood and plaster, bits of candles, tapers, and the ashes of many censers. Behind this, a circular stairway leading to the organ loft. Up this stairway, dust, and a lumber-room containing old chant-books bound in vellum, yellow and worm-eaten, with bronze corners and heavy bindings torn and defaced. Farther on, a small door, and then the organ. The floor was strewn with broken keys, twisted pipes and wire, and the great tubes were smashed in as if with the butt of a musket. I again closed the small door, and descended the stairway. A key grated in a lock, the great door swung open, and let in the sunlight, the hot air, and the sacristan.

Had I been disturbed? Yes, the señorita. He looked startled.

Through which door? Ah! yes; from the

Archbishop's. He had heard about it. It was very sad. The poor señorita, and she so beautiful !

"But is there no hope ? "

"No, mi amigo ; he was shot at daylight."

EL PUERTA DEL VINO. ALHAMBRA
(GRANADA)

THE legends say that the Moorish kings stored their choicest wine in the cellars beneath this curious old archway. It was blazing away this morning at a white heat under a Spanish sun and against a china-blue sky, and it sheltered not the juice of the grape, but an aguador and two donkeys. All three were asleep, — the water-carrier on his back, and the patient, tired little beasts propped up against each other.

They had climbed the long hill of the Alhambra very many times since sunrise, and the water-jars had been often filled that day, and as often emptied into thirsty villagers in the plain below. They had refreshed everybody but themselves. Now it was their turn. So they dozed away, and I continued painting.

If their green jars had contained wine I should have had no use for it. No water-color painter does. But water, pure water, began to be valuable; my bottle was empty, and the well some distance off. It was cruel to disturb them, but after all I am only human. "Agua ? Si, señor." The aguador sprang to his feet, the donkeys lazily opened their eyes, a simultaneous convulsive movement of long ears and short tails, and the procession moved down out into the glare, and halted outside of my umbrella.

A glass wet and held high, glistening in the sunlight, a shower of diamond drops thrown in a circle, a gurgling sound from a cool jar, and, with the bow of an Hidalgo, the aguador handed me that most blessed of all drinks, — cool water in a hot land. I dropped a copper into his outstretched hand, and looked up. He was a tall, straight young fellow, swarthy, with high cheek-bones, and black, bead-like eyes ; a red silk handkerchief bound his head, and a broad sash encircled his waist.

" You are not a Spaniard ? " I asked.

His face flushed, and a smile of supreme contempt crept over it.

" A Spaniard ? Caramba ! No, señor ! I am a gypsy ! Come."

He caught me by the arm, and half dragged me to the low wall which overhangs the plain.

Below was the valley of the Vega and the

city of Granada swimming in a gray dust. He pointed to a narrow road far down the slope, skirted by the river Darro.

" See you those dark holes in the hillside ? That is my home." I made him a low bow. I had not only caught a gypsy, but a cave-dweller.

I remembered instantly that this man's ancestors lived in these holes in the ground before Ibn-I-Ahmar began to build the Alhambra. I also remembered that the Moors had " met with some reverses ; " but here was this sunburnt gypsy living in a house eight hundred years old, and the house still in possession of his family ! I handed him a cigarette, and made room for him under my white umbrella.

His story was very simple. He had been a water-carrier for several years. In the summer time he earned two pesetas (about forty cents). The donkeys belonged to his father, who had half of his earnings. That left one peseta for himself and Pepita.

Was Pepita his wife ? No, not yet, because her mother had been a long time sick ; but soon — perhaps by next Holy Week.

He wished I knew Pepita. " Her waist was so " (making a circle of his two thumbs and his two forefingers), "her ankle was so " (one

thumb and one forefinger), "and her foot so"
(holding up his little finger).

Pepita was as good as she was pretty. Perhaps she would come up to the well to-day, for
she was at mass when he left that morning. He
would go to the well and look for her.

He was gone a long time, and but for the
dozing donkeys broiling in the sun I should have
given him up.

Suddenly four long ears pointed forward, and
two stumpy tails veered like weather-vanes.
Through the archway came my aguador and
the daintiest of little gypsy maidens. She wore
a white kerchief tied under her chin, great
hoops of gold in her ears, strings of blue beads
around her neck and wrists, over her shoulders
a yellow scarf, and on her feet tiny black slippers with red heels. Shading her eyes with her
fan she gave me a timid curtsy, and stood at
one side, resting her hand on her lover's shoulder. She watched every movement of my brush,
and laughed heartily when a few strokes indicated the donkeys.

But it was growing late. Would the most
illustrious painter have any more water? Would
he share the grapes Pepita had brought? Yes,
with pleasure; but Pepita should have five
pesetas.

191

Shall I tell you what happened as I placed the coins in her hands?

"Ah, señor! Bueno! bueno! Mateo, see!" she said, holding up the money and seizing my hand, her eyes filling with tears. Before I was aware she had kissed it.

The aguador leaned forward and whispered, "You know her mother is very sick."

Then he fumbled about between the donkeys, and piled both panniers and all the jars on top of the uglier and sleepier of the two, and the dainty little sweetheart was lifted on the other. Then I watched them through the archway and down the steep hill, until they were lost amid the pomegranates.

I held up the back of my hand. Yes, there was no mistake; she had kissed it. It was a pity that she — but then, of course, I was only a stray painter. I was not an aguador, descendant of a family eight hundred years old, a landed proprietor, with a cash capital of five pesetas, and a half interest in a water-route and two donkeys!

After all, are the good things of this world so unequally divided?

Quien sabe?

A GYPSY DANCE NEAR GRANADA

MATEO, the aguador, and I became great friends. His cheery, bright face, and his welcome "Buenos dias, señor," were very grateful to me so many miles away from home. He and the donkeys stumbled in upon me at all hours, and in all parts of the Alhambra grounds ; and if he did not quickly catch sight of my white umbrella, he would leave his little beasts in the road and go in search of me.

This afternoon I heard his voice far down the hill, and in a few moments more he came singing through the small entrance gate, and, bursting into a laugh, began to tell me the latest news in the city below.

He was especially delighted over the padre who sold the chairs out of the sacristy to the Englishman, and who did not give all the money to the bishop. This I knew to be true, for I had a hand in a similar transaction myself, the chair I write in being part of the villany.

He had a sad story to tell about Santiago, who lived at the great gate, and whose bro-

ther, the matador, had been hurt in the bull-
fight.

Then he told me about the actor from Ma-
drid, who lived in one of the old red towers of
the Alhambra, and who came every summer
with a new wife ; about the mass on Sunday
last, the procession of Holy Week ; and the
great Spaniard who lived in Paris, and who
visited his olive farm only once in five years,
and who arrived yesterday. Then, finally,
about Pepita. I began to notice that all these
talks ended in Pepita. To-day he was in fine
spirits. He had already earned three pesetas,
and it was not yet sundown.

It was a " Fiesta day," and the churches and
streets were full, and the people very thirsty.
To-night he and Pepita would go to the dance.

Up to this time I listened to his talk without
ever looking up from my work. I was struggling with the Moorish arch over the entrance
of the Hall of the Ambassadors, and had my
hands full, but here I laid down my palette.

" What dance, Mateo ? "

" The dance of the gypsies, señor, at the Posada del Albaycin. La Tonta would dance, and
the king of the gypsies would bring his great
guitar. Would the illustrious painter accompany
them ? "

A GYPSY DANCE NEAR GRANADA

That being the one particular thing the illustrious painter most desired to see in all Granada,
I at once accepted, hurried up my work, and
arranged to meet them at the Great Gate of
Charles V. Accordingly about an hour after
sundown I gave my watch and wallet to the
landlord, took my umbrella-staff, and strolled
down the hill.

Mateo awaited me in the shadow of the arch
of the gate, carrying a lantern. Pepita joined
us farther down in the city; she had stopped
on her way up to restring her guitar. In a few
moments more we all halted at the door of a
wine shop in the rear of the church. This was
the Posada del Albaycin. A dim lamp fastened
against the wall revealed a crowd of aguadores,
fruit-sellers, and garlic-venders, together with
a motley crew of Spaniards and gypsies of both
sexes crowding about the entrance.

As I passed in, I heard overhead the click of
the castanets and the low thrumming of the
guitars. Ascending the steps, I found myself
in a long room on the second floor, simply furnished with a row of chairs on either side, and
lighted by a number of lamps suspended on
brackets fastened to the wall. At one end was
a raised platform covered with a carpet. Seated
upon this platform was a man of middle age,

very tall and broadly built, with the features
and expression of an American Indian. Compared in size to the gypsies about him, he was a
giant. He was tuning an enormous guitar, —
a very grandfather of guitars, — having all the
strings which ordinary instruments of its class
possess, and an extra string fastened on an out-
rigger. The back of this curious instrument was
covered with sheet brass.

As we entered he left his chair, placed the
guitar against the wall, greeted Mateo and
Pepita, and, having spoken in an undertone to
the aguador, raised his wide Spanish hat and
saluted me gracefully.

Pepita occupied one of the vacant seats on
the platform, and rested her instrument gently
against her knee, while her lover and I watched
the groups as they crowded up the narrow stairway and filled the floor space.

He pointed out all the celebrities. The tall
man with the overgrown guitar was known as
the king of the gypsies. The dance to-night
was for his benefit. La Tonta was his daughter, and the best dancer in Spain. She did not
dance often. He was sure I would not be dis-
appointed. But the dance was about to begin,
and we must keep silence.

The king bowed to the audience, struck his

guitar with the flat of his hand, swept all the strings simultaneously, twirled it in the air, kissed it, took his seat with a great flourish, and began the melody. Immediately, at the far end of the room, a young gypsy arose, tightened his belt, clapped his hands, and began a slow movement with his feet, the dancers and audience keeping time with their castanets and the palms of their hands.

Then a gypsy girl took the floor and danced a "Bolero." Then came more gypsies in tight trousers and loose jackets, until the hour arrived for the sensation of the evening.

A great clapping announced La Tonta as she entered quickly from a side door, and stood facing the mirror. To my surprise she was a tall, thin, ungraceful, badly formed, and slattern-looking gypsy woman, by no means young. She was attired in a long yellow calico gown hanging loosely about her, much the worse for wear and not overclean. She wore black kid slippers and white cotton stockings. Her skin was dark, like all women of her race, and her eyes large and luminous. Her mass of jet black hair was caught in a twist behind, the whole decorated with blossoms of the tuberose. Taken as a whole, she was the last woman in all Spain you would have picked out as a star danseuse.

197

I looked at Mateo in surprise, but his expression was too earnest and his admiration too sincere. He evidently did not agree with me in my estimate of La Tonta. He laid his hand upon my knee, and said, "Wait!"

At this instant a stout gypsy in his shirt-sleeves, who had been beating time with his cane, and who appeared to be master of ceremonies, cleared the floor, pressing everybody back against the wall.

La Tonta stood surveying herself in the mirror which hung over the mantel. She nodded to Mateo, and began rolling up her soiled calico sleeves quite to her shoulders, revealing a thin, although well-proportioned and not altogether unattractive pair of arms. She then stripped the cheap tinsel bracelets from her wrists, and hid them in her bosom.

As the music increased in volume, she shut her eyes and stretched out her long arms as a panther sometimes does ; then lifted them above her head, and instantly they fell into the rhythm of the music. Her feet now began to move, and a peculiar swaying motion started as if from her heels, ran up through her limbs, back, and neck, undulated through her long arms, and lost itself in her finger-tips.

This was repeated again and again, each

movement increasing in intensity; her eyes flashing with a light rare even in a Spanish gypsy. She stamped her feet, swayed her body backward and forward, almost touched the floor with her hair, and then suddenly rushed forward, appealing to you with her outstretched arms.

The music seemed to possess her like a spell. She became grace itself, her movements sylph-like — and, if you will believe it, positively beautiful. As the music quickened, her gestures became more violent; as it died away, you could hardly believe she moved — and she did not, except the slight shuffling of her feet, which kept up the spell within her.

The effect on the audience was startling. Men rose to their feet, bending forward and watching her every motion. The women clapped their hands, encouraging her with cries of " Ollé ! Ollé ! Brava, La Tonta ! "

Suddenly the music ceased, and La Tonta stood perfectly still. Her eyes opened, her arms fell limp beside her, her back straightened, and she awoke as if from a trance. Giving a quick glance around, she gathered her skirts in her hand, and limped rather than walked through the hall and out into the side room, if anything more awkward than when she had entered.

A GYPSY DANCE NEAR GRANADA

The applause was long-continued and genuine. I certainly did my share of it. The look of supreme satisfaction which came over the face of my aguador as he watched my admiration was not the least part of my enjoyment.

But the dance was over, and we all crowded to the street. Mateo had greetings for his friends, and Pepita was surrounded by half a dozen girls of her own age, who had kind things to say about her part of the performance. In a moment I was singled out and besieged by a bevy of dark-eyed gypsies, who had heard, no doubt, of Pepita's good fortune, and who, if they did not have sick mothers at home, had many other interests which were equally pressing.

" Una peseta, señor," called out half a dozen at once. I had a few small coins left in my sketching-coat, but they were soon distributed. " Por me, señor," said a wicked-looking gypsy girl. My money being all gone, and the bulk of my property being at that moment in the hands of my landlord, I did the next best thing possible. I gave her a red rose from my buttonhole with my best bow. Just here my trouble began. She received it with a cold smile, and turned on her heel. I turned to ask Mateo what had offended her, when a young fellow broke through the group and confronted me, held the rose in his hand, poured out a torrent of abuse, and ground it into the earth with his heel.

Mateo sprang forward and caught him by the throat, and for a moment it looked as if there was going to be as lively a scene as I had ever experienced. But at this instant the powerful form of the king appeared in the doorway, and, after mutual explanations on all sides, the young fellow seemed satisfied that no indignity had been offered his sweetheart, and that the illustrious painter had only intended a compliment especially prized by the señoritas in his own country.

With this we separated, Mateo and Pepita going with me as far as the Great Gate, the groups scattering down the crooked streets, and I to wander about the groves of the Alhambra before going to bed.

It was a lovely night, and I wanted once more to see the Garden of Lindaraja with its deep shadows. A few quick steps brought me beyond the archway of the Gate of Justice, and near the fountains of the Court of Lions.

It was nearly midnight. The Moorish arches, supported on their slender marble columns, wore the color of a tea-rose, as they stood bathed in the moonlight. There was no sound but the gurgling of the water running through the

channels in the marble at my feet, and the regular plash of the fountain.

I began thinking about these gypsies — their
history, the peculiarities of their race, the stories of their villany and treachery, of their vin-
dictiveness, of their curious homes, and then of
this girl whom the music had transformed into
a goddess.

My reverie was broken by the sound of a
footstep, and rising from my seat I looked behind me into the mass of shadow. It ceased,
and I again took my seat. Some visitor, I
thought, who would also see the Alhambra by
moonlight. But I felt uncomfortable. The incident of the rose was, to say the least, unpleas-
ant. I began realizing the lateness of the hour,
and turned my steps back to my lodgings.

On the way home, finding the bucket of the
well of the Moors at the top and full, I had a
cool drink. Then I passed down through the
trees and into the narrow ravine which leads
through the gate, and so on under the archway
and out into the moonlight beyond its black
shadow.

At that instant I became conscious that some
one was following me. I could hear the rapid
footfall timed to keep pace with my own. I
grasped my umbrella-staff, and slid it along my

202

hand until I could feel the iron spike. As I
reached the last outer step of the gate, a man
wearing a gypsy's cloak ran rapidly through
the shadow behind and toward me. I turned
quickly, and recognized the young gypsy who
had so pointedly destroyed my rose under his
boot heel.

At the same instant another figure glided
from the doorway to my side, and said in a low
voice, "Never fear, caballero; it is Mateo. I
am watching the cut-throat."

The gypsy started back, sprang over the low
wall, and disappeared in the darkness. If I
had ever been glad to see Mateo it was at that
moment. He was out of breath — and temper.
For an instant he was undecided whether he
would go home with me or go after the gentleman with the destructive heel. I finally per-
suaded him that he possibly might do both, but
he should leave me at my lodgings first.

On our way down the hill Mateo told me his
end of the story. After leaving Pepita for the
night, and crossing the street which leads to
the Great Gate, he had noticed this fellow
skulking along, and watched him turn into the
Alhambra grounds. Knowing that the gypsy
could not reach his home by that route, and
remembering our recent difficulty, he had

dogged his footsteps into and through the Alhambra, and had caught up with him as I was drinking at the well. Believing that I would go out by the Gate of Justice, he had taken the short cut down the hill, and waited for me under the archway, and I knew the rest.

I reached my lodgings and rapped up the sleepy porter, and bade good-night to my friend the aguador. I hope my additions to Pepita's dowry cured the mother and hastened the wedding.

THE COUSIN OF THE KING

IN Spain evolution has produced the tartana
from the old-fashioned charcoal cart. During the process the cart lost two of its wheels
and the tartana gained two long seats, both
chintz-covered and made comfortable with pew
cushions, besides two pairs of lace curtains
looped back fore and aft, and a brief flight of
steps, farthest from the mule, serving as a sort
of Jacob's ladder for ascending and descending
señoritas.

I was standing in the shadow of one of the
gates of the great Mosque at Cordova when I
saw for the first time a tartana.

It took possession of me, and in five minutes
I had returned the compliment.

It came around the corner with a rush, smothered in a cloud of white dust, in the centre of
which I could see the red tassels of the mule
and the outstretched arm of the driver seated
on the shaft and wielding a whip of convincing
length. Then it whirled around before me,
backed to the sidewalk, and unloaded half a

dozen pairs of black eyes, some mantillas, fans, and red-heeled slippers.

As the fair señoritas were going to mass and I sketching, we separated at once; they disappearing into the cold mosque and I taking their places in the tartana.

A crack of the whip, a plunge from the convinced mule, a dash along a hot, dusty road, bounded by a hedge of prickly pears, and we all stopped at an old Moorish arch, now, as in olden times, one of the city's gates.

I stopped for two reasons. First, because the custom-house officer insisted upon it; and second, because the gate loomed up in such majestic symmetry against the deep blue sky that I determined to paint it at once, and so ordered the driver to unlimber, and prepared for action.

This meant that the mule was unharnessed and tethered in a shady spot, and that I was anchored out by myself in the tartana in the middle of the road, and in the immediate centre of all the traffic of the city's gate.

Any other position, however, would have been useless, for it was the only spot from which I could see through the arch and into the city's streets beyond.

Considering that I and my tartana were public nuisances, the good-nature and forbearance of the populace were remarkable. Every now and then a great string of mules would come to a standstill off my weather bow, the muleteer would slide down from his perch, step forward, peer into my shaded retreat, catch sight of the easel, apologize for disturbing the painter, and then proceed to disentangle his string of quadrupeds as if it was a matter of course and part of his daily routine.

Even the custom - house officers exacting tithes from the hucksters bringing their produce to the city's market, who at first regarded me with suspicion, became courteous and lent a helping hand in straightening out the continuous procession of donkeys, market carts, wagons, and teams crossing the cool shadow of the arch.

The crowd about my muleless tartana were equally considerate. They stood for hours patient and silent, filled my water bottle, brought me coffee, and one old Sancho Panza of a farmer even handed me up a great bunch of white grapes. All they wanted in return was a view of the sketch. This I paid, holding it up regularly for their inspection every half hour.

While this busy scene occupied the roadway under the gate, another of quite a different character was taking place in the grated rooms above it.

I had noticed on my arrival a thinly constructed military gentleman, all sword and mustache, who watched me from a window, and who seemed to take an especial interest in my movements. I now caught sight of him at an upper window gesticulating wildly and surrounded by a group of other military gentlemen, all apparently absorbed in me, my tartana, and my circle of art students. Then they disappeared, and I gave the incident no further thought.

Half an hour later the vista of the street seen through the gate, and consequently the central point of my sketch, was obstructed by a mass of people crowding about the great swinging doors ; and from it marched a file of soldiers under command of an officer, who began a series of military movements of great simplicity.

First they marched up the road and left two men. Then they marched back and left two more. Then they deployed in front and stationed one at each wheel of my tartana, and finally the officer stepped forward, drew his sword, and, looking me searchingly in the face, made this startling announcement : —

" Señor, the general in command has ordered

208

your instant arrest. You will accompany me to the prison."

As soon as I recovered my breath I came down Jacob's ladder and asked politely for an explanation. The only reply was a crisp order closing the files, followed by a forward march which swept me down the dusty road under the gate, through an iron-barred door, up a broad flight of stone steps leading up one side of the gateway, and into a room on the second floor dimly lighted by small grated windows.

As soon as my eyes, dazzled by the glare of the sunlight, became accustomed to the semi-darkness, I discovered an officer with snow-white hair and mustache, seated at a desk and poring over a mass of papers. He was in full uniform, was half covered with medals, and attended by a secretary.

He arose, perforated me with his eye, listened to the officer's statement, and demanded my age, name, and occupation. To these questions I gave civil answers, which the secretary recorded.

Then he faced me sternly and said, "What are you doing in Cordova?"

"A little of everything, your excellency. I prowl about the streets, lounge in the cafés, go

to mass, make love to the señoritas, attend the
bull-fight, and " —

"And make drawings ? "

"I admit it, your excellency."

"What do you do with these drawings, señor
pintor ? "

"Sell them, your excellency — when I can."

"You are a Frenchman ? "

"No, I am an American."

"Your passport."

"I have none."

That settled it. Seizing a pen, he indorsed a
paper handed him by his secretary, passed it
to the officer, and said, in a gruff voice, " Conduct this man to the Governor."

More closing in of files, more drawn sword,
more forward march, and down the stone stairs
we all tramped, out into the glare of the sunlight, through the excited, sympathetic, and
curious mob, and then up on the other side of
the gate, and up a precisely similar staircase,
and into a precisely similar semi-dark room.
More desk, more secretary, — two this time, —
and more excellency, but here the similarity
ends.

At a square table covered with books and papers was seated a young officer, scarcely twenty
years of age, also in full uniform, but without

the numismatic collection decorating his chest. He was occupied in rolling a cigarette.

The only sign he gave of our presence was a glance at the squad and a slight nod to the officer, who saluted him with marked deference. As for myself, I do not think I came within his range.

The cigarette complete, he struck a light, blew a cloud of smoke from his nostrils, read the much-indorsed paper, reached for a pen, and was about to countersign it when I stepped forward.

" Will your highness inform me why I am under arrest ? "

" Certainly ; you have been detected in making plans of this prison, which is a military post of Spain. In time of war this is punished with death ; in time of peace, by imprisonment."

All this, you know, with as much ease and grace of manner as if he had invited me to luncheon, and was merely giving directions about the temperature of the burgundy !

" But I am not a spy. I am simply an American painter travelling through Spain, sketching as I go, and painting under my white umbrella whatever pleases my fancy. Last week it was the awnings over the street of the Sierpes in Seville, yesterday the donkeys dozing in the sun at the gate of the Mosque, and to-day this old Moorish arch, so typical of Spain's great history."

He threw away his cigarette, lost his languid air, took up the paper, re-read it carefully to the end, and said : —

" But you have no passport."

" You are mistaken."

" Produce it."

I ran my hand into my blouse and handed him my pocket sketch-book.

He opened it, stopped at the first page, turned the others slowly, backed unconsciously into his chair, sat down, covered his face with a smile, broke into a laugh, ordered the officer to follow him, and disappeared through a door.

I occupied myself examining the brass numbers on the cartridge-boxes of the squad, and wondering what size handcuffs I wore. Before I had settled it, the officer returned, saluted me, escorted me through the door, leaving the squad behind, and led me into a small room luxuriously furnished. The young Governor came forward and held out his hand.

" Señor, you are free. I have seen your picture. It is admirable. I regret the mistake. The officer will conduct you to your tartana and detail a file of men who will prevent your being disturbed until you finish. Adios."

THE COUSIN OF THE KING

It was a noble and goodly sight to see that awkward squad mount guard in the dust and heat! It was so frightfully hot out there in the road, and so delightfully cool inside the tartana! It was another exhilarating exhibition to watch the crowd and see them tortured by hopeless curiosity to understand the situation. It was still an additional delightful spectacle to contemplate the driver, who had shrunk into a mere ghost of himself when the arrest was made, and who was now swelling with the importance of the result.

An hour later the sketch was finished, the squad dismissed, the officer, who turned out to be a charming fellow, was seated beside me; the mule, the driver, and the tartana became once more a compact organization, and we rattled back through the blinding dust, and stopped at a café of the officer's choosing.

Over the cognac I mustered up courage to ask him this question: —

" If you will permit me, señor capitan, who is the young Governor?"

" Do you not know?"

I expressed my ignorance.

"The Governor, caballero, is the cousin of the King."

A VERANDA IN THE ALCAZARIA

TO really understand and appreciate Spanish life you must live in the streets. Not
lounge through them, but sit down somewhere
and keep still long enough for the ants to crawl
over you, and so contemplate the people at
your leisure. If you are a painter you will
have every facility given you. The balconies
over your head will be full of señoritas fanning lazily and peering at you through the iron
gratings ; the barber across the way will lay
aside his half-moon basin and cross over to your
side of the street and chat with you about the
bull-fight of yesterday and the fiesta to-morrow,
and give you all the scandal of the neighborhood before noon. The sombrerero, whose awnings are hung with great strings of black hats
of all shapes and sizes, will leave his shop and
watch you by the hour; and the fat, good-
natured priest will stand quietly at your el-
bow and encourage you with such appreciative
criticisms as "Muybien," "Bonita, señor,"
"Bonisima."

A VERANDA IN THE ALCAZARIA

If you keep your eyes about you, you will catch Figaro casting furtive glances at a shaded window above you, and later on a scrap of paper will come fluttering down at your feet, which the quick-witted barber covers with his foot, slyly picks up, and afterwards reads and kisses behind the half-closed curtains of his shop. So much of this sort of thing will go on during the day that you wonder what the night may bring forth.

The Alcazaria in Seville, upon the broad flags of which I spent the greater part of three days, is just such a street. It is a narrow, winding, crooked thoroughfare, shaded by great awnings stretched between the overhanging roofs, and filled with balconies holding great tropical plants, strings of black hats, festoons of gay colored stuffs, sly peeping señoritas, fruit-sellers, agua-dores, donkeys, beggars, and the thousand and one things that make up Spanish life.

Before I finished my picture I had become quite an old settler, and knew what time the doctor came in, and who was sick over the way, and the name of the boy with the crutch, and the picador who lived in the rear and who strutted about on the flagging in his buckskin leggings, padded with steel springs on the day of the bull-fight, and the story about the sad-

faced girl in the window over the wine shop,
whose lover was in prison.

But of course one cannot know a street at one
sitting. The Alcazaria, on the morning of the
first day, was to me only a Spanish street; on
the morning of the second day I began to realize that it contained a window over my shoulder
opening on a small veranda half hidden in flowers and palms; and on the morning of the third
day I knew just the hour at which its occupant
returned from mass, the shape of her head and
mantilla, and could recognize her duenna at
sight.

This charming Spanish beauty greatly interested me. If I accidentally caught her eye
through the leaves and flowers, she would drop
her lashes so quickly, and with such a half
frightened, timid look, that I immediately looked
the other way for full five minutes in lieu of an
apology; and I must confess that after study-
ing her movements for three days I should as
soon have thought of kissing my hand to the
Mother Superior of the convent as to this modest little maiden. I must also confess that no
other señorita led me to any such conclusion in
any of the other balconies about me.

On the afternoon of the third day I began
final preparations for my departure, and as

everybody wanted to see the picture, it was displayed in the shop of the barber because he had a good light. Then I sent his small boy for my big umbrella and for a large, unused canvas which I had stored in the wine shop at the corner, and which, with my smaller traps, he agreed to take to my lodgings ; and then there was a general hand-shaking and some slight waving of white hands and handkerchiefs from the balconies over the way, in which my timid señorita did not join ; and so, lighting my cigarette, I made my adios and strolled down the street to the church.

It was the hour for vespers, and the streets were filling rapidly with penitents on their way to prayers. With no definite object in view except to see the people and watch their movements, and with that sense of relief which comes over one after his day's work is done, I mingled in the throng and passed between the great swinging doors and into the wide incenseladen interior, and sat down near the door to watch the service. The dim light sifted in through the stained-glass windows and rested on the clouds of incense swung from the censers. Every now and then I heard the tinkling of the altar bell, and the deep tones of the organ. Around me were the bowed heads of

217

the penitents, silently telling their beads, and next me the upturned face and streaming eyes of a grief-stricken woman, whispering her sorrow to the Virgin. To the left of where I kneeled was a small chapel, and, dividing me from this, an iron grating of delicate workmanship, behind which were grouped a number of people praying before a picture of the Christ. Suddenly another figure came in, kneeled, and prayed silently. It was my timid señorita, and before I was through wondering how she could come so quickly, a young priest entered and knelt immediately behind her. He was the same I had seen in the Alcazaria glancing at her window as he passed.

Fearing that I should frighten her, as I had often done before, I moved a few steps away ; but she was so lovely and Madonna-like, with her mantilla shading her eyes and her fan fluttering slowly like a butterfly, — now poising, now balancing, then waving and settling, — that I instinctively sought for my sketch-book to catch an outline of her pose, feeling assured that I should not be discovered. Before I had half finished she arose, slowly passed the priest, half covered him with her mantilla, and quick as thought slipped a white envelope under his prayer-book !

I PASSED BETWEEN THE GREAT SWINGING DOORS.

A VERANDA IN THE ALCAZARIA

It was done so neatly and quickly and with such self-possession that it was some time before I recovered my equilibrium. Had I made any mistake? Could it possibly be the same demure, modest, shy señorita of the veranda, or was it not some one resembling her? All these Spanish beauties have black eyes, I thought, carry the colors of their favorite matador on their fans, and look alike. Perhaps, after all, I was mistaken.

I determined to find out.

Before she had reached the outer step of the church I had overtaken her, but her mantilla was too closely drawn for me to see her face. The duenna, however, was unmistakable, for she wore great silver hoops in her ears and an enormously high comb, and once seen was not easily forgotten ; but to be quite sure, I followed along until she entered the Alcazaria, and so on to the step of her house. If she touched the old Moorish knocker and rapped, it would end it.

She lingered for a few minutes at the iron gate, chatted with her duenna, watched me cross the street, kept her eyes upon me with her old saintly look, patted her attendant on the back, gently closed the gate upon the good woman, leaving her on the inside, then bent her own pretty head, pushed back her mantilla, showing her white throat, and, flashing upon me from the corner of her eye the most coquettish, daring, and mischievous of glances, touched her finger-tips to her lips, and vanished !

I had made no mistake except in human nature. Surely Murillo must have gone to Italy for his Madonnas. They were not in Seville, if the times have not changed.

I crossed over and had a parting chat with the barber. What about the señorita opposite, who had just entered her gate ? " Ah, señor ! She is most lovely. She is called The Pious ; but you need not look that way. She is the betrothed of the olive merchant who lives at San Juan, and who visits her every Sunday. The wedding takes place next month."

Figaro believed it. I could see it in his face. So, perhaps, did the olive merchant.

I did not.

IN AND OUT OF A CAB IN AMSTER-
DAM

IT is raining this morning in Amsterdam. It
is a way it has in Holland. The old settlers
do not seem to mind it, but I am only a few
days from the land of the orange and the olive,
and, although these wet, silvery grays and
fresh greens are full of " quality," I long for the
deep blue skies and clear-cut shadows of sunny
Spain. On this particular morning I am in a
cab and in search of a certain fish-market, and
cabby is following the directions given him by
a very round porter with a very flat cap and a
deep bass voice.

There is nothing so comfortable as a cab to
paint in if you only know how to utilize its resources. For me, long practice has brought it
to a fine art. First, I have cabby take out the
horse. This prevents his shaking me when he
changes his tired leg. He is generally a spiral-
spring-fed beast, and enjoys the relief. Then I
take out the cushions. This keeps them dry.
Then I close the back and off-side curtains, so

as to concentrate the light, prop my easel up against the front seat, spread my palette and brushes on the bare wooden one, hang my rubber water bottle up to the arm rest, and begin work. (I have even discovered in the bottom of certain cabs such luxuries as knot or auger holes through which to pour my waste water.) I then pass the umbrella staff to cabby, calling particular attention to the iron spike, and explain how useful it may become in removing the inquisitive small boy from the hind wheel. One lesson and two boys makes a cabby an expert. This is why I am in a cab and am driving down the Keizersgraacht on this very wet morning in Amsterdam.

Before the fat porter's directions could be fully carried out, however, I caught sight of an old bridge spanning a canal which pleased me greatly, and before my friend on the box could realize the consequences I had his horse out and tied to a wharf post, and the interior of his cab transformed into a studio.

In five minutes I discovered that a cabless horse and a horseless cab presided over by a cabby armed with an umbrella staff was not an every-day sight in Amsterdam. I had camped on the stone quay, some distance from the street and out of everybody's way. I congratulated myself on my location, and felt sure I would not be disturbed. On my left was the canal, crowded with market-boats laden with garden truck ; on my right, the narrow street choked with the traffic of the city.

Suddenly the business of Amsterdam ceased. Everybody on the large boats scrambled into smaller ones and sculled for shore. Everybody in the street simultaneously jumped from cart, wagon, and doorstep, and in twenty seconds I was overwhelmed by a surging throng, who swarmed about my four-wheeler and blocked up my only window with anxious, inquiring faces.

I had been in a crowd like this before, and knew exactly what to do. Sphynx-like silence and immobility of face are imperative. If you neither speak nor smile, the mob imbibes a kind of respect for you amounting almost to awe. Those nearest you, who can see a little and want to see more, unconsciously become your champions, and expostulate with those who cannot see anything, cautioning them against shaking the painter and obstructing his view.

This crowd was no exception to the general rule. I noticed, however, one peculiarity. As each Amsterdammer reached my window he would gaze silently at my canvas and then say,

223

"Ah, teekenmeester." Soon the word went around and reached the belated citizens rushing up, who stopped and appeared satisfied, as they all exclaimed, "Ah, teekenmeester."

At last commerce resumed her sway. The street disentangled itself. The market in cabbages again became active, and I was left comparatively alone, always excepting the small boy. The variety here was singularly irritating. They mounted the roof, blocked up the windows, clambered up on the front seat, until cabby became sufficiently conversant with the use of the business end of my umbrella staff, after which they kept themselves at a respectful distance.

Finally a calm settled down over everything. The rain fell gently and continuously. The spiral-spring beast rested himself on alternate legs, and the boys contemplated me from a distance. Cabby leaned in the off window and became useful as a cup-holder, and I was rapidly finishing my first sketch in Holland, when the light was shut out, and looking up I saw the head of an officer of police. He surveyed me keenly, — my sketch and my interior arrangements, — and then in a gruff voice gave me an order in low Dutch. I pointed to my staffholder, and continued painting. In a moment

the officer thrust his head through the off window and repeated his order in high Dutch. I
waved him away firmly, and again referred
him to cabby.

Then a war began on the outside in which
everybody took a hand, and in half a minute
more the population of Amsterdam had blocked
up the wharf. I preserved my Egyptian exterior, and proceeded unconcernedly to lay a fresh
wash over my sky. While thus occupied, I became conscious that the spiral-spring was being
united once more to the cab. This fact became
positive when cabby delivered up the umbrella
staff and opened the door.

I got out.

The gentleman in gilt buttons was at a white
heat. The mass-meeting were indulging in a
running fire of criticism, punctuated by loose
cabbage leaves and rejected vegetables, which
sailed, bomb-like, through the air, and the up-
shot of the whole matter was that the officer
ordered me away from the quay and into a side
street.

But why ? The streets of Amsterdam were
free. I was out of everybody's way, was breaking no law, and creating no disturbance.

At this instant half of a yesterday's cabbage
came sailing through the atmosphere from a

225

spot in the direction of a group of wharf-rats, struck the officer's helmet, and rolled it into the canal. A yell went up from the crowd, cabby went down to the water for the headgear, and the owner drew his short sword and charged on the wharf-rats, who suddenly disappeared.

I reëntered my studio, shut the door, and continued work. I concluded that it was not my funeral.

I remember distinctly the situation at this moment. I had my water bottle in my hand refilling the cups, mouth full of brushes, palette on my lap, and easel steadied by one foot. Suddenly a face surmounted by a wet helmet, and livid with rage, was thrust into mine, and a three-cornered variety of dialect that would produce a sore throat in any one except a Dutchman was hurled at me, accompanied by the usual well-known "move on" gesture.

Remembering the soothing influence exerted on the former mob, I touched my hat to his excellency, and said, "Teekenmeester." The head disappeared like a shot, and in an instant I was flat on my back in the bottom of the cab, bespattered with water, smeared with paint, and half smothered under a débris of cushions, water-cups, wet paper, and loose sketches, and in that position was unceremoniously jolted over the stones.

The majesty of the law had asserted itself! I was backed up in a side street!

I broke open the door and crawled out in the rain. His excellency was standing at the head of the spiral-spring, with a sardonic grin on his countenance.

The mob greeted my appearance with a shout of derision. I mounted the driver's seat and harangued them. I asked, in a voice which might have been heard in Rotterdam, if anybody about me understood English. A shabbily dressed, threadbare young fellow elbowed his way towards me and said he did. I helped him up beside me on the box and addressed the multitude, my seedy friend interpreting. I reviewed the history of old Amsterdam and its traditions; its reputation for hospitality; its powerful colonies scattered over the world; its love for art and artists. Then I passed to the greatest of all its possessions, — the New Amsterdam of the New World, my own city, — and asked them as Amsterdammers, or the reverse, whether they considered I had been fairly treated in the city of my great-grandfathers — I, a painter and a New Yorker!

I had come three thousand miles to carry

227

home to their children in the New World some
sketches of the grand old city they loved so
well, and in return I had been insulted, abused,
bumped over the stones, and made a laughing-
stock.

I would appeal to them as brothers to decide
whether these streets of Amsterdam were not
always open to her descendants, and whether
I was not entitled to use them at all times by
virtue of my very birthright. (Another shout
went up, but this time a friendly one.) This being the case, I proposed to reoccupy my position
and finish my sketch. If I had violated any
law it was the duty of the officer to put me
under arrest. If not, then I was free to do as
I pleased ; and if the highly honorable group of
influential citizens about me would open their
ranks, I would drive the cab back myself to
the spot from which I had been so cruelly torn.

Another prolonged shout followed the inter-
pretation, an opening was quickly made, and I
had begun to chafe the spiral-spring with my
shabby friend's umbrella, when cabby rushed
forward, pale and trembling, seized the bridle,
and begged me piteously to desist. My friend
then explained that cabby would probably lose
his license if I persisted, although I might carry
my point and his cab back to the quay.

228

This argument being unanswerable, a council of war was held, to which a number of citizens who were leaning over the front wheels were invited, and it was decided to drive at once to the nearest police station and submit the whole outrage to the chief.

In two minutes we halted under the traditional green glass lamp so familiar to all frequenters of such places. We saluted the sergeant, and were shown up a winding iron staircase into a small room and up to a long green table, behind which sat a baldheaded old fellow in undress uniform, smoking a short pipe.

My threadbare friend explained the cause of our visit. The old fellow looked surprised, and touched a bell, which brought in another smoker in full dress, whose right ear served as a rack for a quill pen, and who used it (the pen, not the ear) to take down our statement. Then the chief turned to me and asked my name. I gave it. This he repeated to the secretary. Occupation ? Painter. "Teekenmeester," said he to the secretary.

Magic word ! I have you at last. Teekenmeester is Dutch for painter.

The chief read the secretary's notes, signed them, and said I should call again in ten days, and he would submit a report.

229

"Report! What do I want with a report, your imperial highness? It is now four o'clock, and I have but two hours of daylight to finish this sketch. I don't want a report. I want an order compelling the pirate who presides over the cabbage market district to respect the rights of a descendant of Amsterdam who is peacefully pursuing his avocation." Certainly, he so intended. I was at liberty to replace my cab and finish my sketch. The officer exceeded his instructions.

But how? I did not want either to provoke a riot or get my cabby into trouble. Ah, he understood. Another bell brought an orderly, who conducted us downstairs, opened a side door, called two officers, placed one outside with cabby and the other inside with me and Threadbare, and we drove straight back to the quay and were welcomed by a shout from my constituents compared to which all former cheering was a dead silence. I looked around for his excellency, but he was nowhere to be seen.

Verily, the majesty of the law had asserted itself!

I do not think I made much of an impression as a painter in Amsterdam, but I have always had an idea that I could be elected alderman in the cabbage market district.

A WATER-LOGGED TOWN IN HOL-
LAND

HAVING shaken the water of Amsterdam from off my feet, dust being out of the question in this moist climate, I have settled myself for a month in this sleepy old town of Dordrecht on the Maas.

It is a fair sample of all Holland, — flat, wet, and quaint ; full of canals, market boats, red-tiled roofs, rosy-cheeked girls, brass milk cans, wooden shoes, and fish. Every inch of it is as clean as bare arms, scrubbing brushes, and plenty of water can make it. The town possesses an old gate built in fifteen hundred and something, a Groote Kerk built before America was discovered, and several old houses constructed immediately thereafter, together with the usual assortment of bridges, dykes, market-places, and windmills.

I lodge in two rooms at the top of a crooked staircase, and as three sides of my apartments overlook the Maas, I see a constant procession of Dutch luggers, Rhine steamers, and fishing smacks. When it rains I paint from one of my windows. When it shines I am along the canals or drifting over to Pappendrecht, or at work under the trees which fringe every street.

My fellow lodgers afford me infinite enjoyment. There is a doctor who does not practise, a merchant who does no business, and mine host who is everybody's friend, and who attends to everything in his own section of the town, including his inn.

Then there is Paul. He is porter, interpreter, guide, boots, railway agent, postal official, head waiter, and cook. He assumes and sustains all these various personages simply by the changes possible with a white apron, a railway badge, and two kinds of cap, — one flat and the other round-topped.

For instance, when you arrive at the brisk little station of Dort, kept permanently awake by the noise of constantly passing trains, Johan is waiting for you, wearing his flat-topped cap and porter's badge, and has your luggage on his handcart before you know it.

Or perhaps at dinner you ask the demure old butler for more boiled fish, and on looking closely and trying to recall his face, you are startled to recognize your friend at the station who handled your trunk. Paul enjoys your puzzled look. He knows it is simply a question of a slightly bald head and white apron in exchange for a flat cap and a badge.

Later on you ask for a guide who speaks your own language, whatever that may be. A jaunty fellow presents himself holding his round-topped cap in his hand, and is prepared to show you the universe. It is Paul.

Besides this, he speaks the fag ends of six languages, all with a strong Dutch accent. He says to me, " It will some rain more as yesterday, — don't it ? " This is why I know he is a linguist.

Last of all there is Sophy, who is maid of all work. She it is who cares for my rooms, sews on my buttons, wakes me in the morning, and washes my brushes. She is a rosy-cheeked girl of twenty, wears a snow-white cap (screwed to her head with two gold spirals), short skirts, blue yarn stockings, and white wooden shoes ; and is never still one minute that she is awake.

Moreover, she has a pair of arms as red as apples and about the size of a blacksmith's, which she uses with a flail-like movement that makes her dangerous. Every paving - stone, doorstep, window-sill, and pane of glass within the possession of mine host knows all about this pair of arms, for Sophy first souses them

with great pails of water, which she herself
dips from the canal, and then polishes them
with a coarse towel until they shine all over.
She has a mortal antipathy to dirt and a high
regard for Paul, whom she looks upon as a
superior being.

These are my simple surroundings in this
water-logged town. I have only one drawback.
I do not speak its liquid dialect.

UNDER A BALCONY

Behind the Groote Kerk is a moss-grown
landing-place, shaded by a row of trees, the
trunks of which serve as moorings for some
broad Dutch luggers floating idly in the sluggish canal. Away up among the branches are
their topmasts, half hidden amidst the leaves.
Across this narrow strip of water is thrown a
slender footbridge to a row of reddish brown
houses running Venetian-like sheer into the
canal, with their overhanging balconies and
windows filled with gay flowers in bright China
pots.

I have already become quite intimate with
the domestic affairs of some of the inmates of
these houses.

One three-windowed balcony especially interests me. I have never seen flowers require so much water. Every time I look up from my easel she drops her eyes and pours on another pitcher. And then the pruning and trimming is something marvellous! She is a bright little body with big blue eyes, and the tangled vines and flowers climbing over the quaint wooden window make a charming frame for her pretty face.

It is difficult to paint under such circumstances, and if I over-elaborated the details of this balcony in my sketch, I frankly say I could not help it.

Suddenly she disappears, and in her place stands a pleasant-faced young Hollander, having the air of a student, who makes me a slight bow which I gladly return, for I am anxious to prove to him how honorable have been my intentions.

In a few moments my fair window-gardener comes tripping over the bridge bearing a small tray, which, to my great astonishment, she lays at my feet on the clean flagging.

She makes no reply to my thanks except with her eyes, and, before I am half through with my little speech, is over the bridge and out of sight.

The tray contains some thin slices of cheese,

235

a few biscuits, and a pot of milk. This is almost immediately followed by the student himself, who holds out his hand heartily, which I grasp, and who addresses me in Dutch, accompanied by those peculiar nods and frowns common to all of us when we are sure we are not understood. I sadly shake my head.

Then he tries Italian. I shrug my shoulders in a hopeless way.

"Perhaps, sir, then, it may be that you speak some English?" I wanted to fall upon his neck.

"Speak English, my dear sir? It is my favorite language. Let us converse in English, by all means. But where did you learn it?"

"Here in Dordrecht. Where did you?"

"I? Oh, in America. My mother spoke it perfectly."

"How interesting! I was not aware you Spaniards spoke it with so little accent. I do not speak Spanish myself, for which I am truly sorry. It is so musical."

Now that was very kind of him. I knew that I had absorbed during my two months' residence in Spain something of the air of an Hidalgo, but I was not prepared for this!

He was glad to make the acquaintance of a Spanish painter. He so much admired our school.

236

He had been in his study and had watched me all the morning, and finding me still at work at lunch hour had taken the liberty of sending his sister with the tray. It was a leisure month with him, the college being closed. He would like to watch me paint, especially now that he knew his own windows formed part of the picture.

An hour later the pretty sister is filling his pipe and my empty cup in a cosy little room with windows filled with flowers, through which I can see my sketching ground of the morning.

She has donned another cap more bewitching than the first, and is busying herself about the room. It is a cosy little den, and rests you to sit in it. The walls are lined with shelves, laden with books. The tables are covered with French, English, and German magazines, pamphlets, and papers. A student's lamp, a few rare etchings, some choice bits of porcelain, and three or four easy chairs complete the interior.

While we smoke my host begs me to tell him something of Spain and my people, and when I undeceive him as to my nationality he laughs heartily, and is doubly glad to make the discovery, for now that he knows I hail from one of the colonies I am of course a kinsman of his. He explains that he had mistaken me for a

Spaniard because as he watched me from his study window he noticed that I smoked cigarettes and twisted my mustache !

Late in the afternoon when I knock the ashes from my third pipe, he insists on accompanying me to my boat, and before we part we exchange cards and arrange for a little dinner at my rooms the next day *for three*.

Verily a white umbrella is better than a letter of credit !

As soon as I reached my lodgings I sent for Paul and handed him my host's card. "Who is that gentleman ? " His eyes opened very wide. "Dot yentleman ? Dot yentleman, Myn Heer, is the professor of English at the University."

A DAY WITH THE PROFESSOR

I tell the professor he is a godsend to me, for while I am all ears and eyes and have something of a nose for poking into odd places, he supplies me with a tongue, which completes my equipment. He returns the compliment by saying I am the only gentleman speaking English he has ever met, and that his pronunciation is improving daily. I remark to him that either Englishmen or politeness have been very scarce in Dordrecht heretofore, at which he laughs and says he shall never overcome all the peculiarities of my language.

Under his guidance I have ransacked every crook, cranny, and sluiceway in this curious old town. This morning being Friday, we go to market. It is a small open square on one side of the Voorstraat. It is really the floor of a great stone bridge, for the canal runs beneath it.

In every town in Holland on market day you will find two stalls which may interest you, — one is the junkman's, who sells old iron, hinges, locks, and broken kitchen ware, and sometimes rusty swords, fragments of armor and rare old brass and copper utensils, battered and bruised. The other contains old books, engravings, and prints.

Successive Friday mornings have added to my own stock of bric-à-brac, but this morning it is the professor who hugs all the way back to my improvised studio three great Dutch books for which he says he has looked for months.

He wondered yesterday why I stopped the milkmaid on the street and bought her heirloom of a milk can, covered with scars and patches and shining like gold, but to-day he is even more astonished at the miscellaneous assortment

239

of rusty iron hinges, locks, and handles I have picked out, and which, with the assistance of an aged locksmith and his wife, will soon be restored to their pristine polish.

But I have an old Dutch cabinet at home which has waited for these irons for years, and the milk can exactly fits the shelf on the top.

He raves, however, about these old books, —tells me that Myn Heer somebody or other, whose name is full of *o*'s and *j*'s, wrote this treatise in the last century, and that there has been a great dispute about it ; that a spurious edition was published which at one time was accepted ; that he had looked for the original for many months. Then he removes his pipe, blows the blue smoke out of my window, and fondly pats the cover.

I think to myself as I look at him, with his high forehead, deep, keen eyes, and thoughtful look, what a thorough Bohemian he would have made if he had only taken to paint and bric-à-brac instead of languages and literature.

The clack of Sophy's wooden shoes hurrying upstairs announces breakfast, which Paul serves with more than usual solemnity, owing to the professor's presence, and also to the fact that for three days no one has arrived at our inn, and consequently his attention has not been diverted from his table to the duties of either porter, railway official, or guide.

This over, Sophy clatters across the clean cobbles to the stone quay, and bails the rain of last night from my boat, and the professor and I drift down the Wagensluis to where some overhanging balconies shelter from the sun and rain an old barge, the bow of which serves as a foreground for a sketch I am finishing of the canal with the Groote Kerk in the distance. While I paint he smokes and reads, and nods to the passing boats, and tells me stories of the people about us and the current gossip of the town, and so the hours slip by.

Then, as the shadows lengthen and my work is over, we row back and out on the broad Maas, and watch the sun set behind the big windmill at Pappendrecht, and the Dutch luggers anchored in pairs in midstream, waiting for a change in the tide to float them to Rotterdam and a market.

When the sun goes down and it becomes quite dark we drift back, picking our way among the market boats moored for the night along the quays, and up to a flight of wooden steps slippery with ooze and slime and well known to both of us. It is the nearest landing to a small beer-house which we frequent.

The landlord greets us heartily, and takes down two pewter-topped mugs from a row against the wall, and spreads a clean cloth over one of the tables overlooking the dark canal, with its flickering masthead lights and deep shadows.

Before we can blow the froth from our mugs the landlord returns with a dish of cold boiled potatoes, some leaves of lettuce, and the castors, and the professor proceeds with great gravity to peel and slice, pour on the oil and vinegar, adding a pinch of salt, and finishing the whole with crisp sprigs of lettuce, which he plants here and there on the top.

A cup of coffee, cigarettes, and pipes, a few strokes of the oars, and I bid the professor good-night at the landing nearest his house, and so on to mine.

Paul thrusts his head from the side window at my third ring, unlocks the door, and lights for me a slender candle. As I climb the crooked staircase, I overhear him yawning and muttering to himself, "Dot veller von America shleep notting."

A VISIT FROM THE DOCTOR

From the windows of my rooms I can see the only busy spot in all Dordrecht. It is the wharf immediately beneath me, where all the Rhine steamers land, and which is crowded all day long with groups of people either going to or coming from the different small towns and villages up and down this outlet to the sea.

On rainy days I draw the curtains wide apart, fasten back the shutters, set up my easel, and pick out a subject from the moving panorama below. The wharf is piled high with garden truck in huge wicker baskets, boxes of fish, rows of brass milk cans reflecting their polished sides in the wet pavements, furniture, crates of crockery, and the usual assortment of small merchandise. On its wet planks the leavetakings and welcomings occur every half hour ; that is, upon the arrival and departure of each boat, and during the whole day it seems as if all the vitality and energy of Dordrecht had concentrated itself under my window. Elsewhere the town is fast asleep.

Out on the Maas the lazy luggers with their red and white sails float by, the skipper's wife usually holding the tiller. Across the marshes the sails of the windmills turn lazily as if it were an exertion for them to move, and over all falls the gentle rain.

On these days I have many knocks at my door, announcing various visitors. The doctor

243

generally drops in early. He is a cheery old soul, and although he speaks very little English, I have picked up enough broken Dutch to piece out with, and so we get on very well. His picturesque faded green coat, yellow nankeen waistcoat, and red necktie make him very valuable around a studio.

Then he is never in the way. He raps, opens the door, sees me, shuts it, raps again gently, and then comes in with an air of surprise mingled with genuine delight at finding me, fills his pipe from my tobacco-box, spreads himself on my lounge, and smokes away quietly.

I should love him for this quality alone, even if he had no other, — for it is a rare kind of man who can come noiselessly into your studio when you are at work, dispense with more than a nod of greeting, slide into a seat, help himself to a pipe, and so unconsciously become one of your surroundings.

Besides, the doctor is especially interested in the small collection of old brass, hammered iron, and bric-à-brac I have made since my sojourn with them all at the inn, and which is scattered about my room, and he takes the greatest delight in examining each new addition that I make.

To-day he is brimful. He has heard of a man

Since then the doctor often starts up from my lounge after a long reverie, knocks the ashes from his pipe, lays his hand upon my shoulder, looks at me sadly, and says, " Dot English-man ! " and then goes out shaking his head ominously. Incidents like these in my quiet life at this charming old inn make even rainy days pleasant in Dordrecht.

UP A BELFRY IN BAVARIA

I AM aware that this is rather an indefinite belfry, for Bavaria covers a wide territory, and belfries are by no means rare; but, nevertheless, this is as near as any one will ever get to the exact locality of this particular belfry from any information which I will furnish, and there are good reasons for my reticence.

This belfry caps the quaint tower of a curious old Franciscan monastery. It is built of red sandstone, seamed and scarred by the weathers of many centuries, and barnacled all over with gray lichen and green moss. It carries within its open arches the remnant of a chime of bells which are never rung, and overlooks a clock which ran down some hundred years ago, and has never been wound up since. Backed up against the wall of this monastery is a small church or chapel. Adjoining the church is a cloister, surrounded by a high wall, on one side of which is an open gate or archway, the whole surmounted by a high peaked roof.

I had walked up from the lower part of the

248

town, where some quaint houses leaning over a narrow canal, reminding one of two old crones gossiping across a street, had tempted me to paint them, and, catching sight of this gate, I loitered in aimlessly. Under the groined arches of the cloister were sheltered idle carts and wagons. From the sculptured tombs in the pavement many restless feet had well-nigh effaced all traces of the graven names of the holy saints who lay buried beneath. It was easy to see that modern Protestantism had no respect for the traditions of the Holy Church.

Crossing the cloister, with its vistas of open squares and small culvert-shaped arches running under rickety houses, I passed a group of heavy columns supporting a low roof, the whole forming a vaulted room. A grated window at one end cast a dim light over an old woman washing. She gazed at me solemnly, and pointed to a door in the wall. Thinking that this was another way out, I turned the knob, and found myself in the refectory of the monastery and confronted by a kindly-faced old friar and a strong smell of cookery. It was some time before I could make him understand how I came there and by what mistake, for my knowledge of German is only that of a traveller. My sketch-book, however, settled

249

it. He turned over the leaves slowly, recognized a pencil memorandum of the gate, took my hat from my hand, hung it on one of a row of wooden pegs, and, motioning me to a seat, dipped a long perforated iron ladle into a steaming caldron, dished out some boiled potatoes and shreds of meat, and placed them on a plate before me. I thanked him and ate my rations like a friar.

Then I followed him through the wide, bare, whitewashed rooms of the ground floor, and into the small church, and such a shabby old church, too! Cheap silvered candlesticks, cheaper cotton lace on the altar-cloth, paper flowers in china vases, ugly modern lamps, German lithographs edged with gilt paper supplying the places of Raphaels and Correggios, and offering-candles, none of which were burning, fastened to iron spikes, from which flowed streams of tallow telling of former prayers. All indicated bitter poverty.

Even the wrinkled old friar seemed a part of the place, — sad, hollow-eyed, and barefooted, his waist bound with a cord from which hung a wooden cross, and he himself as much a tear-stained relic of the past as the walls over which the damp of ages had trickled. Poor old fellow! I can see him now, looking at me wistfully and

250

standing patiently as I examined all he showed me.

Finally he said to me, " English ?" " No," I replied, "American." He dropped the iron hoop which held his keys, and the tears started to his eyes. " American, my son ?" Then he took my hand and by many signs and gestures made me understand that my country was the future home of his church ; that Bavaria in the dim past had seen the grandeur and splendor of the monastery, which had once been heaped full of riches, and had once been proud of its power and prestige, but now she had turned her back upon it and had left it to decay. As he spoke he picked up a small copper censer, poured the ashes out in the palm of his hand, and sifted them slowly on the floor.

I encouraged him to talk, and examined with him the altar screen, faced with a square of some cheap modern fabric, and asked him what it was like in the olden times ? " Velvet and satin, my son, and embroidery of gold and silver ; and the lamps all solid gold ; the walls were cov-ered with paintings, the steps of the altar with fine carpets ; and the Archbishop, to whom the king kneeled, was clothed in lace and scarlet."

By this time we had circled the small church and reached the door, but I was not satisfied.

I led him back to the altar and pointed out the
different objects. Where *now* was the old lace?
Was it stored away somewhere and only shown
to travellers? He shook his head and spread
his fingers as if it had slipped through them
years before. Candlesticks? Lamps? Censers? Still the same mournful shake. All gone.
About the silks and velvets and embroideries
that covered the face of the altar; where now
were they? He simply cast his eyes upward.
But this was a new piece but a few years old;
what was done with the old one? A gleam of
intelligence shot across his wrinkled old face,
and one long, thin finger rested on his forehead.
He looked at me searchingly from under his
bushy gray eyebrows, tapped me on the shoulder, and led the way back through the bare
wide rooms and into the seething refectory, and
up to a row of hooks from which hung keys of
all shapes and sizes. He looked them over carefully, and took down a great hoop linking three
together, lighted a lantern, and I followed him
into the vault-shaped room, past the old woman, who bowed and crossed herself, through
an open court, from which I saw the belfry with
the silent chimes, and up to a door in its tower
heavily grated with iron.

The first key started its rusty bolts, then we

groped our way up a mouldy stone staircase,
the friar going ahead, feeling his way and holding the lantern for me until we reached the
landing of the first story, which I noticed was
level with the roof of the monastery. The daylight, struggling in through diamond-shaped
panes of glass begrimed with dirt and cobwebs,
revealed another door. I looked through its
gratings, but saw nothing but an empty room.
The old friar pressed his shrunken cheek against
the bars, gave a pleased chuckle, unlocked
them, and pointed to a pile of six wooden altar
screens leaning against the wall and half buried
in dust. My heart sank within me.

Not seeing my chagrin he stooped over and
threw down the first screen. A cloud of dust
arose, nearly suffocating me. It proved to be a
worm-eaten frame covered with mouldy canvas. The second, the same; the third, mere
shreds of worsted, with patches of tinsel lace
bearing the figure of the cross embroidered in
faded green. The fourth of silk, threadbare
and stained with the droppings of many candles. As the dust cleared away from each
screen the old fellow would look anxiously in
my face for approval. The fifth — to tell you
the truth, the fifth took my breath away. It
was an old gold-colored corded silk, as heavy

as canvas, and covered with an exquisite embroidery in silk and silver without a break or flaw. The canvas backing had protected it from the damp, and the sixth screen, against the wall, had saved it in a measure from the grime of years.

I broke all the blades of my knife cutting this precious relic of the seventeenth century from its frame, the good friar on his knees meanwhile holding one end taut so that I could run my knife close to the rusted tacks.

His enthusiasm was delightful as he read my face, for the discovery was evidently as much of a surprise to him as to me. " Now I would believe the truth of all the stories of the magnificence of the olden times." And then he lifted it tenderly and carried it as carefully down the treacherous staircase as if it had been blessed by the Pope, and spread it on the grass in the sunlight.

I sat down upon the tomb of an old saint and feasted my eyes.

It was Italian, without doubt, worked in twisted silk and silver in a design of leaves and flowers, the whole in delicate tones of pale yellows, pinks, and turquoise blue. Soiled and stained, of course, but that did not trouble me. I knew a little Frenchwoman near St. Cloud

254

who could take half a loaf of fresh bread and with it work a charm upon its old gold background.

Then I tried a charm of my own with some new gold upon the palm of my old friar. To my surprise he refused it. "No, take it to America. They will appreciate it there. It is nothing here, — all dead, all ashes, all forgotten." Well, then, for the poor? Yes, he would take it for the poor. There were plenty of them always. He would give the money to the bishop for the poor.

As he pressed my hand at the gate his eyes filled, and pointing to the monastery he said slowly, "Never here, my son. In America."

It was not until I reached my lodgings with my prize that I thought of the sixth screen, which in my great joy I had neglected to turn down. What could that have been?

This question I am not yet able to answer, and until I am I shall not tell anybody where in Bavaria is my belfry.

THE END

255

𝕮𝖍𝖊 𝕽𝖎𝖛𝖊𝖗𝖘𝖎𝖉𝖊 𝕻𝖗𝖊𝖘𝖘

Electrotyped and printed by H. O. Houghton & Co.
Cambridge, Mass., U. S. A.

www.ingramcontent.com/pod-product-compliance
Lightning Source LLC
Chambersburg PA
CBHW020616260626
47157CB00003B/1039